TABOR EVANS

LONGARM

AND THE PAIUTE INDIAN WAR

JOVE BOOKS, NEW YORK

THE BERKLEY PUBLISHING GROUP
Published by the Penguin Group
Penguin Group (USA) Inc.
375 Hudson Street, New York, New York 10014, USA
Penguin Group (Canada), 10 Alcorn Avenue, Toronto, Ontario M4V 3B2, Canada
(a division of Pearson Penguin Canada Inc.)
Penguin Books Ltd., 80 Strand, London WC2R 0RL, England
Penguin Group Ireland, 25 St. Stephen's Green, Dublin 2, Ireland (a division of Penguin Books Ltd.)
Penguin Group (Australia), 250 Camberwell Road, Camberwell, Victoria 3124, Australia
(a division of Pearson Australia Group Pty. Ltd.)
Penguin Books India Pvt. Ltd., 11 Community Centre, Panchsheel Park, New Delhi—110 017, India
Penguin Group (NZ), Cnr. Airborne and Rosedale Roads, Albany, Auckland 1310, New Zealand
(a division of Pearson New Zealand Ltd.)
Penguin Books (South Africa) (Pty.) Ltd., 24 Sturdee Avenue, Rosebank, Johannesburg 2196,
South Africa

Penguin Books Ltd., Registered Offices: 80 Strand, London WC2R 0RL, England

This is a work of fiction. Names, characters, places, and incidents either are the product of the author's imagination or are used fictitiously, and any resemblance to actual persons, living or dead, business establishments, events, or locales is entirely coincidental.

LONGARM AND THE PAIUTE INDIAN WAR

A Jove Book / published by arrangement with the author

PRINTING HISTORY
Jove edition / April 2005

Copyright © 2005 by The Berkley Publishing Group.

ISBN: 0-515-13934-3

JOVE®
Jove Books are published by The Berkley Publishing Group,
a division of Penguin Group (USA) Inc.,
375 Hudson Street, New York, New York 10014.
JOVE is a registered trademark of Penguin Group (USA) Inc.
The "J" design is a trademark belonging to Penguin Group (USA) Inc.

PRINTED IN THE UNITED STATES OF AMERICA

10 9 8 7 6 5 4 3 2 1

PUNISHMENT SERVED

"Well, well," Jake said, slowly getting to his feet and rubbing blood from his nose onto his sleeve. He spat onto the palms of his calloused hands. "What do we have here? A real fighter, huh?"

"Come and get your dessert," Longarm taunted.

Jake pulled a wicked knife from his boot top. "Maybe I'll just slit your throat," he said.

Longarm glanced at Spike Drummer, but the man wasn't about to interfere. Rather, there was a wild look of feral anticipation in the rancher's face that was almost more chilling than Jake's gleaming knife blade.

Longarm looked around for a weapon or something to help him fend off the knife attack, but saw nothing. And so, as Jake closed in for a killing thrust, Longarm crouched low, grabbed a handful of dirt and sand, and then hurled it into his attacker's eyes.

Jake was momentarily blinded, but he bulled forward, knife slashing. Longarm grabbed the big foreman's wrist and tried to twist the knife loose, but failed. They grappled and wrestled, then Longarm slammed his hip into Jake and threw the big man to the ground. He jumped on Jake, still intent on disarming the man, but they rolled. Longarm felt the knife blade sear his chest, but then he got the upper hand and bent Jake's wrist around.

It was over in the split second that it took for Longarm to throw all of his weight and strength onto the knife, burying it into Jake's belly.

DON'T MISS THESE
ALL-ACTION WESTERN SERIES
FROM THE BERKLEY PUBLISHING GROUP

THE GUNSMITH by J. R. Roberts
Clint Adams was a legend among lawmen, outlaws, and ladies. They called him . . . the Gunsmith.

LONGARM by Tabor Evans
The popular long-running series about Deputy U.S. Marshal Long—his life, his loves, his fight for justice.

SLOCUM by Jake Logan
Today's longest-running action Western. John Slocum rides a deadly trail of hot blood and cold steel.

BUSHWHACKERS by B. J. Lanagan
An action-packed series by the creators of Longarm! The rousing adventures of the most brutal gang of cutthroats ever assembled—Quantrill's Raiders.

DIAMONDBACK by Guy Brewer
Dex Yancey is Diamondback, a Southern gentleman turned con man when his brother cheats him out of the family fortune. Ladies love him. Gamblers hate him. But nobody pulls one over on Dex . . .

WILDGUN by Jack Hanson
The blazing adventures of mountain man Will Barlow—from the creators of Longarm!

TEXAS TRACKER by Tom Calhoun
Meet J. T. Law: the most relentless—and dangerous—manhunter in all Texas. Where sheriffs and posses fail, he's the best man to bring in the most vicious outlaws—for a price.

Chapter 1

It was autumn in Denver and brightly colored leaves were sailing from the cottonwoods that lined Cherry Creek as United States Deputy Marshal Custis Long strolled beside his latest girlfriend, Miss Lilly Hutton. Because it was Sunday, and the weather was ideal, the winding dirt path that they followed was busy. Laughing children played hide-and-seek while parents sat on the riverside or picnicked on patches of grass. A few people were fishing but without much success, and several teenagers were flying kites, which bobbed and ducked on the upper thermals.

All in all, Custis Long thought it was a perfect Sunday afternoon to be out with a young woman so lovely that she attracted smiles from every man they passed.

"So," Lilly said, "you'll be staying in Denver for awhile."

"I expect that I will," Longarm told her. "This last trip to Arizona was hard. I had to track some train robbers out of Yuma into the heat of the desert. Chased them nearly to New Mexico."

"How many were in the gang?"

"Four."

"Did they surrender without a fight?"

"No," Longarm said, watching two derelicts slink into the riverside thickets for no reason that he could imagine. "They had killed the train conductor and knew they'd hang if I took them back to Yuma. So they laid a trap for me in the badlands. I was using an Apache and he saw the trap and we circled around behind and got the drop on them."

Lilly waited. Finally, she said, "And then what?"

"The Apache and I ambushed and killed them all."

"Oh," Lilly said, her eyebrows arching in surprise. "I thought you were supposed to arrest criminals whenever possible."

"You are," Longarm said. "But the Apache and I knew these men would never give up, so we did what we had to do."

"I see." Lilly looked troubled. She was, Longarm knew, a woman who had seen little or no violence. Unlike Longarm, who had fought in the Civil War and had known hard times since as far back as he could remember in West Virginia, Lilly was the daughter of a well-to-do merchant. It was also no secret that her parents did not appreciate their daughter being in the company of a rough frontier law officer. They'd never said as much to Longarm, but their disapproval of him was clear and strong.

Longarm paused and stared at the place where the pair of derelicts had disappeared. Such men were not unusual here and he knew that many of the dregs of Denver lived in the brush and thickets along the creek. Mostly, they were a sad and harmless lot who spent their days drinking cheap liquor and quarreling among themselves. Sometimes their quarrels escalated into real violence and the police were called into these hidden encampments to retrieve wounded or dying men, usually those cut up in vicious, drunken knife fights.

"What are you staring at?" Lilly asked.

"Did you see those two men that disappeared into those thickets?"

2

"Yes. I feel sorry for that type. They have no homes, you know." Lilly shook her head in sadness. "They are underfed and uncared for. I don't know why their families don't rescue them from such poverty. Whatever do they do in the wintertime when it gets freezing cold?"

"They move closer into the city," Longarm said, his mind still focused on the thickets. Perhaps he should have ignored the pair, but he had sensed something about their movement that spelled trouble. The pair had not just been moving toward their own camp, they had been sneaking up on someone, and Longarm knew that did not bode well.

"I give to the local charities all that I can afford," Lilly was saying. "I know that some people think that these derelicts are simply lazy and shiftless, but I believe that we ought to show them more compassion. Don't you, Custis?"

He thought he heard a muffled cry of pain, muffled voices filled with fear and distress.

"Lilly," he said, "I want you to stay right here on this footpath in plain sight of people."

"What . . . ?"

"Please do as I say. I have a bad feeling something is going wrong in those thickets and I need to investigate. It might be nothing at all but . . . well, I have a gut feeling that something sinister is happening."

"All right." She tugged momentarily at his coat sleeve. "Please be careful. I've read that some of these poor derelicts are deranged, and territorial. They don't like people not like themselves coming into their camps."

"I'll be careful."

Just then, Longarm heard a louder cry. Or rather, a shriek.

He broke into a run and plunged into the thickets. Now he could hear the sounds of a violent struggle taking place back deeper in the thickets.

Because he was going out with a lady on a sunny Sunday afternoon and did not want to further incite the displeasure of Lilly's judgmental parents, Longarm had left his sidearm, a double-action Colt Model T.44 caliber revolver in his room. He did, however, carry a twin-barreled derringer of the same caliber that was affixed to his watch chain and rested hidden in his vest pocket. The derringer was very inaccurate beyond twenty feet, but in close quarters, it was deadly.

"Hey!" he shouted, bursting into a small and littered encampment where the two derelicts he'd seen were now standing over two other homeless and apparently injured souls. "What's going on here?"

The aggressors whirled and Longarm saw that they both had knives, the blades of which were covered with blood. One of them, a large scarecrow of a man with bad teeth hissed, "This ain't none of your affair, mister. You'd better get out of here or you'll get the same as these two."

Longarm's eyes went to the pair on the ground and he realized that they were silver haired. One of them appeared to have been hurt quite badly and was moaning. The other lay still and bathed in his own blood.

Longarm drew his badge and said, "I'm a United States marshal and you men are under arrest. Drop those knives."

"He ain't packin' a gun," one of them said to the other. "The bloody fool is unarmed!"

"Drop the knives and raise your hands," Longarm ordered, taking a few steps closer to the men. He replaced his badge in his pocket. "Don't make things even worse for yourselves by resisting arrest."

"Jake," the smallest of the pair asked. "What are we gonna do? He's a lawman and we . . ."

"Shut up. I'm thinkin'."

"Well think faster, Jake."

Jake was even taller than Longarm, but he was thin. His long face was smeared with grease and dirt and there was a terrible scar that started at his neck and disappeared into his beard.

4

Longarm moved closer to the old pair sprawled on the ground beside a big cottonwood tree. Then he said to the attackers, "Did you stab and rob them?"

"Officer, we just found those two old drunks lyin' here on the ground hurt and we were fixin' to help them."

"Sure you were," Longarm said. "Now for the last time, drop those knives and raise your hands!"

"Jake? What are we gonna do?"

The tall men exposed all of his bad teeth and said, "I see a gold chain and I'll bet the lawman has some money. Ain't that right, Marshal?"

"That's right," Longarm said. "But the real question is . . . are you stupid enough to try and take it?"

Jake crouched and his partner did the same. Jake hissed, "You know how this works, Marvin. We done it enough times before."

"But this is a *marshal!*" the smaller man protested. "I think we oughta just get out of here."

"Not without what we came to find," Jake spat. "Now, let's carve this lawman up and get on with our business!"

"You're both making a bad, bad mistake," Longarm warned.

But Jake wasn't listening as he and his friend began to separate and move in for the kill. Longarm waited until the two men were within six feet and he could smell their stink before his hand slipped into his vest pocket and he pulled out the short and deadly little derringer. He had figured this would stop them cold, but Jake was already lunging at him, so Longarm shot the tall man squarely in the chest.

The explosion was loud and Jake stood up straight with the knife still clenched in his fist, his eyes turning downward to see the rose blossoming darkly across his chest. Then he lifted his eyes to Longarm and choked, "You didn't even show us your gun."

"Sorry," Longarm said, turning his pistol on the smaller man, who had dropped his knife. "Don't kill me, Marshal!" he begged, releasing his bladder so that the sharp odor of urine filled Longarm's nostrils. "*Please* don't."

Longarm glanced at the man's pant leg and saw yellow water trickling across on his scuffed boot. "Turn around and lie on the ground with your arms and legs spread-eagle. If you move, I'll put a bullet in the back of your head."

"Yes, sir!"

Longarm went over to the victims. He was saddened that they were just two old men. He knelt beside one of them and said, "Mister, where are you cut?"

"All over. I'm dyin'."

Longarm tore open the man's shirt. He had seen a lot of wounds in his time and his first impression was that, if he could get the bleeding stopped, this man still had a fighting chance. What was working against him, however, was that he was old, undernourished and in extremely poor physical condition.

"What's your name?"

"Bert."

"And your friend?"

"His name was Jimmy Watson." Bert grimaced and shuddered. "We protected each other for all these years. Used to be buffalo hunters down in the Kansas country. Got out and the buffalo all got shot out. Now we got nothin' but sorrow."

Jimmy wasn't breathing, and when Longarm tore open the man's ragged coat, he saw that he'd been stabbed just below the ribs, a perfect thrust up into the heart.

"You need a doctor," Longarm said, turning back to Bert. "You're losing too much blood."

"Is Jimmy gone?"

"I'm afraid so."

Tears filled the old man's eyes and he began to weep. Longarm whirled around and went over to his prisoner. "Did you put the blade to Jimmy's heart?"

"No, sir! It was Jake. Jake was the one that stabbed and cut them two old men. I didn't want him to do it. I just . . ."

6

"Liar!" Bert screamed. "You was in on it just as much as the other. You killed me and you killed Jimmy! Jumped us when we was drunk and sleepin'. That's what you boys did, all right!"

Before Longarm could get to his prisoner, Bert rolled to one side, grabbed a gun from under a filthy blanket and opened fire. There wasn't a thing that Longarm could do as the wounded old man emptied his gun. Longarm could probably have used the second bullet in his derringer, but it wasn't in his heart. This, he thought, was simple justice.

"There," Bert said, still pulling the trigger on spent cartridges. "I guess that will show 'em not to sneak up on a pair of old drunks and cut 'em to ribbons. I hope they're both already burnin' in hell!"

Longarm placed his hands on his hips and gazed down at Bert. "You could go to prison for murder."

"I ain't gonna live long enough to get there," Bert whispered. "Besides, Jimmy's gone. He's the only friend I had in this world. Why don't you just go away and let me bleed to death, Marshal."

"Because I can't," Longarm told the old man. "I'm going to try and stop the bleeding now."

"Too late," Bert whispered. "I ain't got so much blood in me anymore. Just foul water and whiskey. Marshal, I got a bottle over there by that pack. Do an old man a mercy and give it to me so I can have me one last drink before I leave this wicked world."

Longarm hesitated, but when he studied the light that was fading in Bert's bloodshot eyes, he made his decision and retrieved the bottle of cheap whiskey. "Here. Drink your fill, Old Timer. Did either you or Jimmy have any kinfolks that I should notify?"

"No, sir. I got no money, either. I guess Jimmy and me gonna be put into a pauper's grave, huh?"

Longarm saw no sense in lying. "Probably so."

"No fancy walnut casket with brass trimmings. Proba-

7

bly just a bed sheet instead of even a clean smellin' pine box. But, Marshal, it don't matter," Bert said, taking a long, desperate pull on his bad whiskey. "Rich or poor, I believe we all go on to a far better place."

"Custis?"

He turned around to see Lilly standing in the clearing, her hands up covering her mouth and her eyes wide with shock.

"Lilly, I think you'd better go back where I left you and wait."

But the young woman came forward one slow step at a time. "What happened?" she whispered.

"I'll tell you later. There's nothing that you can do here right now. And you don't need to see this, Lilly. You don't need to at all."

But Lilly kept advancing until she was standing beside him and then she knelt beside Bert as he whispered, "Lordy, I must have just got in to heaven for I see an angel appearing before me!"

Lilly choked back tears. "I'm no angel, Sir. Are you . . ."

"But you *are* an angel," Bert whispered with his last breath of life.

Tears streamed down Lilly's cheeks and a sob escaped from her that nearly tore Longarm's heart out. He bent down and raised Lilly up. "Let's go," he said. "I'll get hold of the authorities. They'll take care of this, but I'll have to fill out reports. Lilly, I'm afraid our day together is over."

She nodded, unable to take her eyes off Bert. "Do you really think he believed I was an angel?"

"I do," Longarm said. "And what better thing could you have done for Bert than to appear as an angel?"

Longarm folded Lilly into his strong arms while he surveyed the campground and the four dead men. Even if Lilly had been Bert's angel, there was no way that this bloody campground could ever be mistaken for heaven.

Chapter 2

The following Monday morning, Marshal Billy Vail leaned back in his leather office chair, brow furrowed, fingers drumming his desk. Suddenly, he got up and went to his window where he could look out at the nearby Denver Mint and then down on busy Colfax Street.

Where was Deputy Marshal Custis Long? He was supposed to be here for a meeting at nine o'clock but it was almost ten now and the tall deputy marshal had yet to make his appearance.

Billy frowned. Custis was his best officer, but the man had no concept of time, and he was anything but punctual. Still, not one of his deputies was as successful in the field. Billy knew that, whatever shortcomings Custis Long might possess, the man was smart, fearless and incorruptible.

Suddenly, Billy spotted Longarm striding along the avenue with a gorgeous young woman on his arm. The day was blustery and the woman's black hair was giving her fits, although she was doing her best to hold down her wide-brimmed and stylish hat. Even at this distance, Billy could see that she was gorgeous and petite. She looked like a young society girl, which was surprising because Longarm generally associated with a lower class of female.

But, when it came to members of the opposite sex, Longarm was quite egalitarian . . . he loved and appreciated them all.

"Maybe this is the one," Billy said to himself. "She is as fresh and lovely as a rose in the morning dew."

Billy smiled as the couple stopped at the base of the federal building. Longarm, tall and handsome, removed his snuff-brown hat, bent over and kissed the woman lightly on the lips. She turned her face upward and Billy suddenly caught the sheen of tears on her cheeks.

"You cad!" Billy swore from his upper story window. "What have you said or done to this angelic girl?"

Billy watched the couple part when Longarm disappeared into the federal building. And while he shouldn't have cared, Billy felt upset that his deputy had been the cause of the girl's tears. Longarm, a Southerner who possessed both chivalry and refined manners, could be a bit on the rough side. Billy supposed his deputy had to be that way in order to have survived all the perilous frontier assignments he'd taken in the line of duty.

Still, Billy resolved to find out why the lovely young woman had tears on her cheek and then sternly reprimand his deputy.

Five minutes later, Billy opened the door to his spacious office and said to his aged secretary, "Remind Deputy Marshal Long that he had an appointment with me this morning an hour ago. Furthermore, tell him that, if he is not in this office in one minute, he will face . . ."

Billy paused.

"Face what?" the aged and widowed secretary asked, trying to suppress a smile. "Are you going to *fire* Longarm? Take his badge and send him packing, Mr. Vail? Or perhaps just dress him down a little and hope he doesn't burst out laughing."

Her name was Miss Edna Dorfney and she was small, plucky, irreverent and the best secretary in the entire Federal Building. Edna had worked here for nine years and was known for her sharp tongue, honest opinions and sterling work ethic. Still, there were times when Miss Dorfney really could rankle Billy and seemed almost insolent. Times like right now, as she stood waiting with a half smirk for his answer as to just what discipline he would administer in retaliation for Longarm's habitual tardiness.

"Miss Dorfney," Billy said, making a lame effort to retain his authority and dignity "just . . . just tell Custis to get into this office at once!"

"Of course, sir. At once."

Billy returned to his desk. Most of his deputies were punctual and they were excellent report writers. They called him *Mr.* Vail and were respectful. They even remembered to bring chocolates on his birthday and to inquire about his wife and children. But not Longarm. No, Custis Long treated Billy . . . not as his boss . . . but his friend and equal. And for reasons he could not understand, chubby, over-the-hill and out-of-fighting-shape Billy Vail loved Custis Long for that.

"Good morning, Billy!" Longarm said, cheerful as usual. "Did we have a nine o'clock meeting this morning?"

"Yes we did. You know that we did."

"Ah, dammit, I forgot."

"No," Billy corrected as he leaned back in his leather office chair, "you didn't forget, you just didn't care."

"Ah, Billy! That's not true."

"It is true."

"No it isn't."

Longarm was smiling and it was hard to stay mad at someone who smiled at you. Billy gave it up and said, "How was your weekend?"

"Interesting."

"Your whole life is interesting. Any new prospects?"

Longarm knew that Billy, being happily married, for some reason wanted the same for him. Wanted it rather badly, although Longarm could not understand why. Marriage was for later . . . maybe . . . because it tied a man down something awful. And to make matters worse, it usually involved having children. Longarm didn't exactly dislike children, but he much preferred them to belong to someone else. Someone middle-aged, in a safe job and comfortable like Billy.

"No prospects," Longarm assured his boss once again.

Billy wasn't pleased with this answer. "I . . . uh . . . just happened to see you on the street down below with a very attractive young woman. A woman whose dress and demeanor suggested that she was of some breeding and refinement."

"Oh? How interesting."

"Don't be a smart-ass, Custis. This girl wore a lavender dress and matching hat. Beautiful, with pink roses. She had the shiniest black hair and a lovely face, almost classic Grecian, I think."

"You don't miss much, do you, Boss? Given your excellent salary, I'd have thought you'd have more important things to do than to gaze out the window on a Monday morning."

"I was waiting for you. Remember?"

"Sorry."

"Now, about that young woman you kissed on the stairs below."

"Billy, just let it alone."

He knew Custis did not like anyone to delve into his romances. Still, since Longarm had more romance in his life than any ten other men in the building, Billy was insatiably curious.

"Is she new in your life?" Billy asked shamelessly.

"Yes," Longarm said, knowing the man would not be satisfied until he had a few details. "I've only known her for two weeks."

Billy raised his eyebrows and grinned. "Well, I must say

12

that she is certainly a cut above your usual, shall we say, earthy type."

Longarm had not taken a seat. Now he reached over to pluck one of Billy's good cigars. "Is this what the meeting was to be about? My latest lady love?"

"Love?" Billy scoffed. "That's a joke. I mean, Custis, have you ever loved a woman? I mean, *really* loved her?"

"Yes. As a matter of fact, I have."

"Who and when?" Billy demanded.

"My mother when I was a child."

Billy snorted. "That is not at all what I meant and you know it. And why was that lovely creature crying?"

Longarm drew a small silver knife from his pocket, snipped off the tip of Billy's fine cigar, gave it a good sniff and then asked for a match. When he had the cigar going he took a seat and inhaled with a sigh. "Billy, you have great taste in cigars. Is this Cuban?"

"Don't attempt to derail the former line of inquiry. Why was that girl crying? What did you do or say to such a refined and lovely soul?"

Longarm's smile faded. "We were walking along the pathway by Cherry Creek yesterday when a crime was committed."

"Serious?"

"Very," Custis said. "Two old and harmless derelicts were savagely attacked by men with knives. Both old men died and Lilly, I'm sorry to say, witnessed their violent passing. The blood and heinous acts very much upset her. Being of a delicate nature, it will take some time for her to recover. The entire thing was savage and regrettable. That was the cause of her tears."

"And the perpetrators?"

"I shot one them as he attacked me with a knife. The dying old man shot the other."

Billy leaned back in his chair. "So all *four* are dead?"

"Afraid so," Longarm said. "I thought that one of the victims might survive, but he had lost a great deal of blood. Furthermore, with his old friend and companion dead, he seemed to have lost the will to live."

"Then did you notify the local police?"

"Of course," Longarm said. "But first I escorted Miss Lillian Hutton home. I called on her this morning and tried to raise her spirits but she was still quite shaken. Also, I can assure you Lilly's parents were not too pleased with me."

Billy leaned back and straightened his tie. "Her father wouldn't happen to be Arnold H. Hutton, president of the Bank of Denver?"

"Yes," Longarm said, "I believe he did tell me that. All I know is that he's quite the stuffed shirt and doesn't much care for my attentions toward Lilly. Mrs. Hutton is also cool and disapproving."

"I should think so," Billy said, quite delighted with this situation. "The Huttons are very prominent and wealthy. No doubt they had expected their beautiful daughter to set a bit higher standards for a suitor and prospective husband."

"I'm not a prospective husband," Longarm said, a little annoyed at the insult. "I'm just her current fella."

"What could you possibly have in common?"

"Are you implying that, because I lack social status and money, I'm unworthy of Miss Hutton?"

"No, no," Billy said quickly. "Not at all. But you come from such very different backgrounds. She, one of wealth, you . . ."

Longarm inhaled deeply. "Billy, you know that I come from West Virginia. Correct?"

"Yes."

"But have I ever told you about my background and family?"

"No, although I have always been curious."

"Well," Longarm said, "it might surprise you to know that I did come from a family of some wealth and position.

14

By that I mean that I was not raised a poor, ragged farm boy who spent his youth behind a mule and a plow."

"I never supposed you were a farmer's son."

"Listen," Custis said, wearying of this personal conversation. "I find Lilly . . . Miss Hutton . . . a very charming and wonderful person. What we have in common is a love of beauty and laughter. And the reason she seems to find me attractive, I think, is because I represent excitement."

"And this young woman yearns for excitement?"

"Yes," Longarm said flatly. "She has lead a very sheltered existence. Lilly feels stilted and oppressed. She and I do things together that are adventuresome and . . . well, perhaps you would say forbidden to most girls in her position."

Billy's eyes widened. "You're not . . ."

"Not yet," Longarm said, knowing exactly what Billy had in mind. "But, if Lilly decides she wants to be loved by a man who can teach her the joys of lovemaking, then I certainly won't refuse her desires."

"Custis! That poor girl would be like a rabbit being ravaged by a wolf! You must not ever compromise her virtue."

"Is this conversation over? And didn't we have a nine o'clock meeting for some useful purpose other than your prying into my romances?"

Billy blushed. "Yes. As a matter of fact we do have serious business to discuss."

"And that is?"

"Your next assignment."

"Billy," Longarm protested, "you promised me at least two weeks of vacation. I haven't had any vacation this entire year and all the assignments you've given me have been unusually dangerous and demanding."

"That's because you are the only one under my authority whom I trust explicitly. Who can handle the tough jobs."

"Don't try to flatter me into taking another job like the one I just finished down in Yuma."

"I have another job for you . . . one that will require all the resourcefulness and ability you have to offer."

"Where?"

"Northern Nevada."

Longarm nodded. "That's one of my favorite places."

"I know that," Billy said. "And this case involves a railroad and several murders. And, of course, the theft of U.S. government bonds."

"Deputy Marshal Murray handled something like that in Kansas. Why not send him before he gets so fat he can't climb on a horse?"

"This case is far more complex and dangerous."

"Billy, I *need* two weeks of vacation. Can't this wait?"

"I'm afraid not. Take care of it and I promise I will give you a month off."

"Put that in writing?"

"Yes."

Longarm began to pace the room. "I don't know," he muttered. "I hate to leave Lilly while her mind is so agitated. I need at least a few days with her. The young lady needs a strong shoulder to lean on right now . . . and I'm it."

"Humph! About that I really wonder."

"Meaning?"

"Never mind. You can have three days and then you must leave for Nevada. And, frankly, I will use those three days to gather all the additional information I can by telegraph. I don't want you going into an Indian war without . . ."

"What *Indian war?*"

"Well," Billy hedged, "that part of it doesn't sound like much."

"How could an Indian war not be much?" Longarm demanded. "Who is it, the Paiutes, again? Or the Shoshone?"

"We're not sure. There have been some raids and scalping. The usual stuff."

Longarm shook his head and started for the door.

"Where are you going?"

"I've got three days with Miss Hutton," he replied. "I'll see you on Thursday morning at nine o'clock, and kindly have a little more information about the little 'Indian war' and the train robberies and murders. OK?"

"Sure," Billy said. "I'll pull everything I can get together and have your travel money ready so you can catch the train that afternoon."

"Make it generous," Longarm said. "Or I might decide to ask Miss Hutton to marry me and make me a rich husband."

Billy laughed but Longarm wasn't even smiling as he left the man's office. Indian war? Murder on trains? Well, at least it sounded challenging.

Chapter 3

Longarm and Lilly were sitting in one of Denver's nicer restaurants, having just finished lunch, when Lilly set down her glass of iced tea and said, "Custis?"

"Yes?"

"Today is our last day before you leave for Nevada."

"I know." He shrugged. "Duty calls."

She propped her chin on her hands, leaned across the table closer to him and said, "You don't seem nearly as upset about this parting as I do."

"Oh, but I am!" he protested. "Leaving you is very hard. I'll miss you very much. You'll be on my mind every minute I'm away."

"You don't *have* to go."

"I'm afraid that I must."

"Custis, I confronted my parents about us last evening after you took me home from the theater."

Longarm took a deep breath. He didn't like the way that this conversation was moving. "Now why did you do a thing like that? You know they'll never approve of me. It's better just to let it alone. Perhaps, in time, they'll resign themselves to me, but don't count on it."

"They already have accepted you," she told him. "I explained that we were madly in love."

He searched his pockets for a cigar and realized he was all out. His mouth felt dry and he was starting to get a pounding headache. "You did?"

"Yes. And I told them that you were the only man that I would ever love and that they might as well get used to the idea."

Longarm shifted uneasily and reached for his glass of iced tea. "Lilly," he began, "I don't see the point in upsetting your parents. And maybe we're rushing this just a mite. I mean, we've only known each other for about a month."

"Thirty-three days."

"Well, OK," he told her.

"Custis, I told them that I fully intended to marry you."

He spilled his iced tea on his lap, mopped up the mess and then pressed the cool, damp napkin to his brow. "I didn't think we'd talked about marriage."

"No, we haven't," she agreed. "So let's talk about it right now."

He glanced furtively around at the other customers, who most certainly were leaning toward Custis' table, straining to eavesdrop. "Maybe we should go somewhere else if we need to talk about this."

"Fine," she agreed. "Let's go."

Longarm laid some cash on the table and glared at the people who had been eavesdropping. "Sorry to leave you hangin', folks," he muttered as he followed Lilly out the door into the bright but windy afternoon.

"It's a little blustery to talk in the park," Lilly said. "So let's go to your apartment. I haven't been there yet and I do so want to see it before you leave for Nevada. But I'm not convinced that you really must leave and that's what I want to talk about."

"There's nothing to discuss, Lilly. It's my job. Like I said, duty calls."

"We'll see about that."

Longarm had been with dozens of attractive young women who had mistakenly thought he would settle down and marry them. That he would meekly accept a desk job and wear a suit and tie. And so he could now easily recognize that Lilly was going to put full pressure on him *today.* By the firm and determined set of her jaw, he could see that she was resolved to make him cancel his Nevada assignment, quit the federal government, and take up a dull, but socially acceptable and better paying profession right here in Denver.

"Lilly," he said, "there's a great exhibition over at the art museum we talked about seeing and . . ."

"Custis, you're not even slightly interested in art. You would be bored silly, so why bother?"

Why indeed, Longarm thought.

"But my apartment is an unholy mess. It's cluttered and there are dirty dishes in the sink and unwashed clothes scattered about on the floor. Lilly, I'm just too ashamed to have you see it. My unimpressive little apartment is a hovel. A cave. A dirty den where . . ."

She silenced him with her sweet lips. "It's a part of you that I want to know, Custis. Besides, I would love to help you neaten it up. And, of course, you won't be staying there much longer."

"No?"

"Of course not. After we're married we'll find a big, fine home to buy. Now, let's go straighten your 'dirty den' up."

"But I don't want it straightened up."

"Also, I'd like to cook you dinner tonight. Do you have a stove and any food in your icebox?"

"No. Not a morsel. Not even enough to satisfy a mouse."

"No matter," she said breezily. "We'll buy something nice at the grocery and I'll prepare you a delicious supper."

"You can cook?"

"Well, I'm going to learn," she said quickly. She shrugged her shoulders. "Of course, we've always had a cook at home, but I have watched her make a few things and I'm game to try, if you are."

"I'd rather go out tonight."

But she wasn't listening. "We'll have wine . . . no, champagne!"

A street beggar that Longarm always helped appeared before them, but Longarm's scowl was so pronounced the beggar wisely turned away. "Lilly," he said, "champagne is for celebrating. What's to celebrate about our separation?"

"That's one of the things we are going to discuss," she said, dashing into a grocery store that advertised fine wines and liquors.

Longarm stood on the street corner, waiting and worrying. He was afraid that Lilly Hutton was absolutely committed to domesticating him, no matter how much he resisted.

"There!" she said, coming out with several bottles of expensive wine and champagne. "Plenty for dinner and for celebrating."

"Good," he said, taking the sack. "My apartment is just two blocks away. Couldn't you wait here for about an hour while I straighten it up a bit? Maybe you'd like to shop for whatever it is that you insist on cooking."

"I'll shop a little later after I see what you have to go with what I have in mind frying or boiling."

"But . . ."

She slipped her arm though his arm. "Stop fretting so, Custis! I've seen dirty rooms before. I had an older brother. He was such a pig that father sent him off to a military academy. Unfortunately, he caught the croup and died there. He's buried in the academy's cemetery and they even gave him some sort of a medal, though they never explained what he did to earn it. Poor, slovenly Marvin."

"You never mentioned him."

"We don't speak his name in our house. He was fat, mean and rather homely. I would never say this to Father, but I am sure that Marvin was also depraved and sexually perverted."

Longarm's eyes widened and he waited for Lilly to elaborate, but she didn't. Instead, she just kept walking and seemed entirely too happy for Longarm's liking.

"All right, Lilly," he said, taking a deep breath as he unlocked his apartment door. "I want you to promise me that, if it's too disgusting, you'll tell me so and we can leave at once."

"It will be fine," she replied, not looking quite so sure anymore.

It was a one room, second floor apartment located in a brick building. Its best attribute was that the landlord admired Longarm and made sure that the security was always tight. No stranger got past the landlord's first floor apartment without being stopped and questioned. Also, the rent was cheap and the building was in one of the better parts of town, close to Longarm's favorite saloons and eateries.

Longarm swung the door open and an angular tabby tomcat that he had befriended and who cleaned his dishes with his raspy tongue let out a hiss and disappeared through a partially open window.

"Who was that?"

"Herman the cat. We're old friends. He stays with me when I'm in town. When I leave on an assignment, he disappears and lives off the street. We admire each other's *independence*."

Lilly stepped into the apartment. "It's not so bad," she said, trying to sound cheerful. She walked over to Longarm's dresser and smiled at the disarray, then ran a finger across its dusty surface. "Why, with a little dust on everything, you can even write messages to yourself!"

Longarm hastily collected some of his underclothes. There wasn't much he could do with the kitchen, with its litter and unwashed dishes and utensils. At least Herman had done his part in the cleanup.

"I'll open a bottle of wine," Lilly told him. "Do you have a corkscrew?"

"There's one around here someplace. I don't use it much. I usually drink whiskey."

While Longarm rummaged through his tiny, messy kitchen, Lilly strolled a few feet over to his bed, which was unmade. She happened to glance down and saw that he'd missed picking up a piece of underwear. To her shock and surprise, it was a pair of lace panties.

"Oh," she said, lifting them with the very edges of her fingernails. "You forgot something here."

He whirled around and gulped. "Ha! Herman drags the damnedest things in here while I'm gone."

"Yes, I can see that. Did you find the corkscrew?"

Just then he did find it. "Ah, yes! Let's open the bottle."

They opened the bottle and while Lilly cleaned two unmatched water glasses, Longarm made sure that there were no other pieces of women's underwear to be discovered.

"To us," Lilly said, raising her glass in a toast. "And to our future together as man and wife."

Longarm's glass was half raised when she added the 'man and wife' thing and it made his hand tremble. "To us," he said.

They drank, then Lilly refilled their glasses and raised them again. "And to your new profession."

"What!"

She took a deep gulp and motioned for him to do the same. Longarm emptied his glass, not at all comfortable with the way this was going. "Lilly, what do you mean 'new profession'?"

24

"Like I said, I had a long talk with my parents about you last evening after you dropped me off at the house. And I'm happy to say that they are willing to rethink things about us. They even admitted that you are a handsome fellow and probably have some brains and ambition."

"How flattering," he deadpanned.

"Yes," she said, cheeks glowing with excitement and from the wine. "And when I told my father about you leaving for another dangerous assignment in Nevada tomorrow, he surprised me by saying that I could offer you a job at his bank. That way, you don't have to go!"

"Now, Lilly . . ."

"Custis, hear me out. This isn't just some hack teller job. It will be a good job with real responsibility and a very good starting wage."

"Doing what?"

"My father wasn't sure, but he told me to tell you that he would think of something. Maybe in security."

"You mean I would stand around all day in the bank's lobby and, in the unlikely case the bank were to be robbed, it would be my responsibility to thwart the holdup."

"Well, I told him you were fearless and good with guns. A dead shot and brave under fire."

"Thank you," Longarm said, "but I don't think I'm interested."

"All right then," Lilly said, taking a generous swallow, "I'll push him for something even better. And it doesn't have to be with the bank. My father owns or has financial interests in many Denver businesses. Why, he could even lend you money to start your *own* business, once we're man and wife."

"Lilly, I think this conversation is . . ."

"Darling," she said, leaning over and kissing him wetly. "Don't be a complete fool and throw this opportunity of a lifetime away! Together, we can work out something that you'd do well. With all my father's connections and money,

25

you could not possibly fail. And then we could have a lovely home . . . my father would probably buy it . . . and lots of love and children! We'd have everything."

He could see how very much she wanted this and he was both flattered and touched. "Lilly, you are beautiful, kind and intelligent. But I'm not ready to get married."

"But I *love* you! Don't you love me?"

"Why . . ." he cleared his throat. "I'm not quite sure. Of course, I think a great deal of you. But the truth of the matter is you're really quite far above me, Lilly. You could have your pick of Denver's rich and successful young bachelors. Respectable men who have gone to prestigious universities like Harvard and Yale."

"But I don't care a fig about that." Lilly drained her wine glass. "Do you think you are *close* to loving me?"

"I think . . ."

"Shhh! I think I know what the problem is. You are afraid that I'm too innocent. Too naive. That you'll shock me with the sordid truth of your past. But you won't, Custis. I know that you've slept with a hundred or more whores and floozies."

"I have never paid a prostitute," he interrupted. "But I have . . . well, I have slept with many women. Some of them were decent, some indecent. However, that isn't the point."

Lilly wasn't listening. "I want you to know that I am a *passionate* woman. I have enough passion for you to satisfy your every whim and desire."

"Lilly, I'm leaving for Nevada in the morning. Perhaps we should go out to dinner. Have a nice time and then reflect about things while I'm gone."

"I have something you need to know. I had a dream a few nights ago. A terrible, horrible dream that you were killed in Nevada."

Longarm felt a shiver travel the length of his spine. And although he did not want to know, he felt compelled to ask, "How did I die?"

26

"You were chased down by Indians. They shot arrows into your body then split your skull with an ax and you were scalped, but even so still half alive. I woke up screaming, trying to save you, Custis."

Longarm was very nearly fearless but this kind of talk gave him the spooks. "It was just a dream. A figment of your imagination. We all have nightmares and we need to push them aside realizing they mean nothing."

She was not persuaded. "Some of my dreams have turned out to be prophesies. I can't explain it, but they have. Usually the worst ones, too."

Longarm didn't want to talk about this anymore. It might jinx him, fatally. "I need something stronger than this wine," he said abruptly as he jumped to his feet, tossed what remained of his wine out the window into the alley and then found a bottle of good whiskey.

"I'll take some of that, too," she said, pitching her wine after his. "Be generous."

Longarm was generous filling both glasses. He was beginning to wish he had not insisted on having three more days to share with Lilly before leaving Denver.

As he viewed it now, just two days would have been much, much better.

"Lilly, what are you doing now?"

She tossed a big swig down her throat and giggled. "I'm getting undressed and going to bed with you, silly."

"You're what?"

"You heard me."

"But you're not that kind."

"Not yet I'm not." Lilly was swiftly undressing and what Longarm could see was eye-popping. "But I've waited for you too long. Waited for any man too long." She hiccupped and he realized that the wine and whiskey were going to her head, making her bold and uninhibited.

"Lilly," he said, struggling, "I think you are about to do something you might regret."

27

"Nope! Come on, Big Boy! Show me the way to paradise and then I'll show you why you can't possibly leave tomorrow on that train."

She was completely naked now and he was gaping . . . and stiffening.

"Come on!" she said, her eyelids shuddering, her lips puckered and her body starting to undulate like that of an exotic belly dancer. "Have you ever had a *virgin* before?"

"Uhh, I don't think so."

"Well you are now!"

She hopped into his bed and wiggled all over like an excited puppy. Longarm had the feeling this was going to get him into even more trouble than he could handle. But there she was and here he was and . . . what the hell? She wasn't going to be a virgin forever!

When he mounted Lilly there was a gasp of pain, then a sigh and a growl from deep in her throat. "You're so big I feel like you're going to split me in half. Oh, this is . . ."

"What?" he asked anxiously. Longarm had never hurt a woman in his life and he sure wasn't going to start now.

"Good! What should I do now?"

"I'll do everything," he told her as his right hand moved expertly down her belly. "And then you'll know what needs doing without being told."

Lilly was already showing signs that she was a fast learner. Longarm buried his face between her lush breasts and did what he could do so well. In minutes, Lilly was going crazy and Longarm was grinning from ear to ear. It hadn't been since he was about thirteen years old that he'd had a real, honest-to-goodness virgin.

"Oh! Oh!" Lilly was howling, her heels wildly spurring the bed, balling up his dirty sheets. "Why did I ever wait so long!"

Custis couldn't and wouldn't even attempt to answer that. All he could do was to make sure that Lilly was broke in right. That she knew from the start how a good man ought to make love to a good, passionate woman.

And if, god forbid, he did get scalped and axed by the Indians in Nevada, at least this was going to be a great last night in Colorado.

Chapter 4

Lilly was in tears the next day when Longarm stood on the train loading platform and gave his ticket to the conductor. People were staring and they probably thought he was an insensitive beast who had committed some outrage against this lovely young lady.

Longarm couldn't help what they thought, and frankly, he did not give a damn.

"Custis," she said, sniffling. "Last night you said that you'd come back and then we could really talk about getting married."

"I did?" Longarm couldn't remember that discussion, but a man making love to a woman could be excused for promises he probably couldn't or wouldn't want to keep.

"Yes, and I'm holding you to it," Lilly pronounced. She dried her eyes and blew her nose. She fumbled for something in her purse. "I want you to think only of me when you are in Nevada. And I want you to have this gold necklace as a reminder of our love."

Longarm stared at the chain and beautiful jewel pendant. The stone was red, slightly opaque and set in solid gold. It was large, about half the size of a silver dollar. "It's beautiful."

31

"Do you like it?"

"Sure, but it is a *woman's* jewelry."

"Custis, it's an exceptional garnet and it is very lucky. It saved my grandmother's life when she fell into the ocean and it saved my mother's life when she choked on a chicken bone in Boston."

Longarm did not particularly want to know the details. "Lilly," he said, quite touched. "It's an heirloom and you should keep it. Because where I'm going people would kill for the gold setting alone. And I could lose it."

But she shook her head. "It will save you from *death*. If you wear it, I'll sleep easy until you return to my arms and . . . and everything else you discovered last night. Please do this for me, if not for yourself."

He couldn't say no. "All right."

"Will you telegraph me when you reach Elko in Nevada?"

"What for?"

"You know my address. Have your messages delivered in an envelope marked PERSONAL. I just want to hear from you, that's all."

And before he could object, she shoved a wad of money into his coat pocket. "Keep in touch, *please*."

"Lilly, I . . ."

"All aboard!"

Longarm kissed her and then, just to make her feel better, he slipped the necklace and precious garnet over his neck and down under his collar. What the hell?

"Thank you and come back soon!"

He was exhausted from their night of lovemaking and tripped on the steps, nearly falling to the cinders. But the conductor caught his arm, and he jumped up on the train just as it was pulling away from the platform.

Longarm stood waving at Lilly while the train gathered speed, heading north to Cheyenne, where he would transfer to the Union Pacific. He absently touched the unfamiliar piece of jewelry hanging around his neck and smiled.

"Maybe I will think about marrying that girl," he said to himself. "A man could hardly do better."

"Your wife?" the conductor asked, following Longarm's gaze.

"Perhaps someday."

"She's a pretty filly. But once they tie you down and start having babies there goes their looks and all the romance."

"Really?"

"Trust me." The conductor had a white walrus mustache and looked to be about seventy years old, but he had a twinkle in his blue eyes. "My wife was shaped like that young beauty when we met forty-five years ago, but now she's as big around as a sow with a hide to match."

Longarm was a bit startled by this man's frankness and lack of sentimentality. "Well, we all get old."

"You can say that again. And when they get kids, they forget about you. All you're good for then is bringing home the bacon. They got your paycheck spent before you even take off your tie. Money. That's what they all start thinking about after they catch a husband."

"Oh," Longarm said, still watching Lilly recede into a dot. "I wouldn't have to worry about that. Miss Hutton's father is rich."

"Jeezus," the conductor whistled through some missing teeth. "That's the *worst* kind to marry!"

"Why?"

"Because you can never match up to the father. You're always just a toady suckin' hind tit. You'll never be good enough and they'll bring up their fathers and tell you that to your face. I sure wouldn't marry a rich man's daughter." The sour old conductor shook his head emphatically. "No, sir! You'd always be suckin' that hind tit."

Longarm had heard about enough. According to this

33

jaded geezer, if you married a poor woman, all she wanted after children was your paycheck. And it was even worse if you married a rich one. Longarm decided the conductor was just fed up with matrimony and probably should have stayed single all his life.

"Well, I'll go find my seat and get some sleep."

"You look awful tired. Been up all night doin' the bump with her and sayin' good-bye, huh."

Being a gentleman, Longarm didn't answer.

"Lucky bastard," the conductor wheezed as he wandered off down the aisle to collect tickets.

The trip up to Cheyenne had been pretty uneventful except for a woman bound for San Francisco.

"My name," she said, when she met Longarm in the aisle after heading west out of Cheyenne, "is Pomona Durado. I'm not Mexican or Italian but pure Spanish. My grandfather had a rancho in the Sacramento Valley. But the Americans took it away and now my family owns a shipyard in Vallejo."

"Where is that?" he asked.

"Near San Francisco."

"I've never been there. Pomona is a very interesting and unusual name. What does it mean?"

Her eyelashes fluttered slightly and her lips parted to reveal perfect white teeth. "It's Latin and means Goddess of Fruit. But I prefer just to be called Mona."

"How interesting," he said, thinking that it was a perfect name for a woman of such succulence. She had a heart-shaped face, high cheekbones and long, lustrous black hair. She also had full lips and beautiful brown eyes. From the neck down, things looked every bit as enticing.

Mona asked, "How could a man like you not have seen such a place as San Francisco?"

Longarm didn't have a ready answer for that one. "Actually, I've only been up into the Sierra Nevadas. Lake

Tahoe is one of my favorite vacation spots. But I've never been all the way down into California. I hear that it is extremely hot and humid."

"Hot yes, humid, no," Mona said. "By the way, I'm in first class."

"I'm in the coach car, unfortunately."

"What a shame," she said, those full and inviting lips making a sensual pout. She wore a pair of lovely jade earrings and a matching necklace that Longarm guessed was worth at least a year of his salary. Everything about the woman spelled money as well as smoldering passion. "I've seen the coach cars and they are primitive and very uncomfortable."

He shrugged. "I'll survive."

"How far are you going?"

"To Elko, for starters. After that, I don't know."

"Elko?" She made a face to show her disapproval. "That is not much of a town. Just dust, cattle and grass. Are you a cowboy or rancher?"

"No," he said, "I'm a United States deputy marshal out of Denver."

Mona's eyes dropped. "And I bet you carry a *big* gun."

Her meaning made Longarm's cheeks warm and spoke volumes about the woman. Like Miss Hutton, Mona was rich but that was where all the similarities ended. Mona Durado was a man-eater if he'd ever seen one.

"It was nice making your acquaintance, Miss Durado. And I hope you have a pleasant journey in first class."

"I get bored. Maybe you'd like to come and see me this evening."

"I'd better not."

"Why? I won't hurt you. We can just . . . talk. And besides, traveling in coach is horrid. You know that as well as I do."

"Yes," he admitted, "it's not exactly pleasant."

"Then do come and see me this evening. We can share a

35

bottle of wine and a few stories. Are you married or engaged?"

"No."

"Then what could be the harm?"

Longarm thought about the miserable conditions in coach. The hard seats, the noise, the rancid smell of long-unwashed bodies, the dust and the bare-bones surroundings. "Maybe I will," he heard himself say.

"Then I'll see you later, Marshal."

He watched her turn and stroll up the aisle just like every other man in sight did. Longarm shook his head and went back to his seat in the coach car. It was a rough way to travel, but it was all that the government would pay when it sent a mere deputy marshal across country. Billy Vail and those bureaucrats above him would have wangled a first-class ticket, especially on such a long and boring journey westward. And, as Longarm sat down in his hard wooden seat and listened to the crying of children and the snoring of unwashed men, he considered what it would be like to have money. The kind of money that marrying Lilly Hutton would bring.

Suddenly, two out-of-control children were running up and down the aisle, screaming and wrestling. Next to him, a man with his mouth hanging open was snoring so loudly that he could be heard despite the noisy and rambunctious children. In the seat directly behind Longarm, a baby had messed its britches, and it smelled awful. Flies buzzed and someone farted loudly.

Longarm tried to open his dirt-streaked window to get some fresh air, but it was sealed.

Longarm was repelled and disgusted. A drunk staggered up the aisle, drooling and muttering obscenities, and then disappeared into the toilet area and the end of the car. You could hear him violently vomiting.

I don't think I can stand this for the next thousand miles, he thought. *And besides, Mona said she was lonely and just wanted to talk. That wouldn't be cheating on Lilly, would it? Of course not! And besides, Mona was right. I'm not married or even engaged. I'm a man and I can do whatever I want as long as it's legal and hurts no one.*

His mind made up, Longarm decided that he could hardly wait to get out of his miserable surroundings and go visit the woman in first class.

Chapter 5

Longarm had no trouble finding Miss Pomona Durado's first-class sleeping compartment early that evening. He had purchased a bottle of excellent brandy in the dining car, although it cost more than he should have spent, and it was to be delivered along with a red rose and two snifters by the porter soon after his arrival.

"Come in!" Mona said, smiling warmly. "I have been waiting for you."

The compartment was nicely appointed. The walls were covered with a polished mahogany veneer and there were two small seats that Longarm knew could be folded into a good-sized bed. There were overhead compartments where luggage, pillows and extra blankets were stored. It was cozy and seemed downright elegant compared to the miserable coach car where Longarm was forced to endure not only a grubby collection of fellow passengers, but also a total lack of privacy.

"I've got the porter bringing us refreshments," he said, just a moment before the man appeared with the brandy, rose and glasses on a handsome wooden platter.

"What a nice thing to do!" Mona said. "But you really shouldn't have."

"Why not?"

She took the rose, inhaled its perfume and said, "Because I already had this railroad's finest Southern whiskey brought by the porter."

Longarm shrugged. "It's a long, long journey," he said, thinking that he wasn't going to be able to resist this woman's obvious physical charms. "I'm sure we can work our way through both bottles by the time I get off this train in Nevada."

"So which shall it be this evening?" she asked. "Brandy or whiskey? What is your pleasure?"

Longarm didn't hesitate. "Whiskey."

"That's what I thought you'd say." She opened the bottle and poured. "To a pleasant journey west and to our new friendship."

Longarm drank to that and then asked, "Why me?"

"What do you mean?"

"Why did you pick me to come here instead of someone else?"

Her answer surprised him. "I watched you at the Denver train station through the window. I saw that young woman and tried to imagine what was passing between you during the good-bye."

"And?"

"I had the feeling you were unsure of your feelings toward her, but that she was deeply in love with you. She was quite beautiful, and unless I am sadly mistaken, well to do."

"Her father is quite wealthy," Longarm said.

"So why wouldn't a poorly paid lawman want a beautiful and wealthy woman?"

"I like my freedom," he said without hesitation. "I like what I do and am not ready to settle down into being a husband."

She smiled. "So you're a very independent man who isn't dazzled by a woman's beauty or money."

"I guess not, although I admire both."

Mona raised her glass. "And that is *exactly* the impression I had of you in Denver. And, quite frankly, I find that very rare and honorable."

"And that's why you chose me to join you this evening?"

"That and the fact that you're hands-down the most handsome man on this train. What more reason should I require?"

Longarm had to chuckle. "I don't know. I'm just glad to be here instead of in coach. And I'm glad that you understand that I have no interest in a long-term affair."

"Nor do I, Marshal."

"Just call me Custis."

They raised their glasses to each other again and Longarm was beginning to think that this trip might be a whole lot more interesting and pleasurable than he'd even hoped.

"Do you enjoy reading books?" she asked.

"Some."

"I just finished *Ben-Hur* by Lew Wallace. "It's a wonderful historical romance about the Christians in the time of the Roman Empire. I couldn't put the book down and I cried when it ended."

"My favorite author is Mark Twain," Longarm said. "*The Adventures of Tom Sawyer* is a personal favorite, although I really enjoy going back to *Roughing It* every year or two. That guy has a great sense of humor and his descriptions of both people and places are pure genius."

"Yes," she said. "He came to California and the Sierra mining camps. Wrote a tongue-in-cheek piece about some leaping frogs that became quite famous."

"That he did."

From there the conversation moved on to politics, which held no great interest for Longarm. Politics had gotten him into the horror of the Civil War, and to his way of thinking, politics were the cause of half the world's problems. But Mona enjoyed talking politics. The year before, James Garfield had been elected president by a very narrow margin, but had served less than one year when he was assassinated by a disgruntled and probably insane minor office-seeker. Garfield's successor, President Chester Arthur, was widely thought to be an incompetent buffoon.

"It's a tragedy," Mona lamented. "What's to become of this country under such a man as President Arthur?"

"It'll survive, just as the country survived Lincoln's assassination."

"Two presidential assassinations in less than two decades," Mona lamented. "Custis, if I were a prominent national politician, I'd never seek the office of the President of the United States. I'd be too afraid of being shot by some demented zealot."

"I would be, too."

"And what will become of the assassin?" she asked.

"Unless Charles Guiteau's defense lawyer can convince a jury that he is completely mad, Guiteau will be tried, convicted and hanged," Longarm said with conviction. "Any less a sentence than death, and the public will riot in the streets all across America."

"Have you seen many hangings?"

"Too many," Longarm told the woman.

"They must be terrible to witness."

"They're never pretty, but sometimes, if the crime was especially heinous, I almost feel like applauding when the trapdoor falls and the hangman's noose closes."

"Do the victims . . ." Mona gulped her whiskey. "Do they suffer when hanged?"

Longarm thought about that a moment before answering. "If the hangman does his job properly, the drop breaks the neck, and death is instantaneous. Sometimes, however, the act is botched and the condemned man slowly strangles, and his face becomes so discolored and distorted in agony that it is always wise to put hoods over the man before his execution."

Mona shuddered.

"How horrible."

"Yes, but most condemned suffer most *before* they are hanged," he told her at last. "Waiting is worse than death itself. I've seen prisoners try to kill themselves rather than take their last walk up to meet the hangman. I've seen them go insane and turn into babbling idiots so that they really didn't know what was happening to them when they were carried up the gallows."

Mona shook her head. "I'll never understand the mind of the murderer."

"No one really does," Longarm said. "From my professional observations, I think people kill for all kinds of reasons. And, often afterward, they even manage to judge themselves innocent. They come up with the most creative ways imaginable to justify their murderous acts. Men kill wives and then swear they did it because their spouses were cheating on them. Or women kill their husbands and claim it was done in self-defense . . . and it often was."

"Have you ever seen a *woman* hanged?"

"Once," Longarm said. "But she looked and acted like a man. Mrs. Eunice Tumbull split her husband's head wide open with a meat cleaver, claiming self-defense. But she outweighed her husband by fifty pounds and her neighbors all testified that she was as mean as any viper. A unanimous jury found her guilty and she was sentenced to be hanged. Big, strong farm woman who cursed the crowd, the judge and everyone she ever knew, including her children, until her very last breath. When she dropped . . ."

Longarm could not finish.

"What?"

"You don't want to know."

"What!"

43

"The hangman messed up and Mrs. Tumbull's head detached."

"Oh my god!" Mona drained her glass. "How did we ever get onto this morbid subject?"

"Beats me," Longarm said. "Let's talk about something else."

So they talked for several hours about many things small and often funny. As the hour grew late, Longarm saw that they were already on the western slope of the Laramie Mountains, heading into Laramie.

The trip was going nicely.

"I'd better go," he said sometime after midnight.

"Why don't you stay?"

"Are you sure?"

"Very." Mona removed her jade jewelry and then her blouse. "Life is short," she told him. "Why don't we make the most of it?"

"Why not?" he agreed.

Moments later, he and Mona were arranging the seats into a nice, comfortable bed and then tearing off their clothes. Mona was almost as lovely naked as Lilly had been, and for a moment Longarm felt a pang of guilt. But then she was all over him like a tiger and Longarm was equal to the challenge. Mona was anything but a virgin and she enjoyed a rough and tumble coupling. When she finally cried out with ecstasy, Longarm wondered if the people in the adjoining compartments could hear their passionate lovemaking. But then he decided that they could not because of the pounding of the rails.

So he forgot about that and kept up his own pounding.

"I need to go back to coach," he told her afterward.

"Why on earth would you want to do that at this hour?"

"I left some things in my seat that I don't want stolen." He buttoned up his pants and reached for his shirt. "I'll get them and return very soon."

Mona Durado gave him kiss and yawned. "Hurry back."

"I will."

Longarm wasn't gone fifteen minutes, but when he returned to Mona's first class coach, he found her door slightly ajar.

"Forgot to tell her to lock it," he muttered to himself.

"Mona, I'm back," he said, stepping inside.

The light was dim, just as it had been when he had left Mona. But there was enough light to see that everything else had changed in his brief absence because their cozy little love nest had been ransacked and turned upside down.

And there lay Miss Durado with a knife buried in her chest and those once-stunning eyes now staring up at the ceiling.

"Miss Durado!" he shouted, rushing to her side and yanking out the offending blade of a big pocket knife. "Mona!"

She had only been dead a few minutes and the blood was fresh. Longarm jumped back out of the apartment for an instant to see if the killer was still in sight, but the aisle was empty. Then he went back inside the compartment and cradled the naked and still-warm body in his arms. He had forgotten to close the compartment's door and heard a hysterical screech.

Longarm glanced aside to see a heavyset woman filling the doorway. She was dressed in a pink flannel nightgown, her eyes bugged out in horror, and screaming, "You *killed* her! Murderer! You *killed* her!"

"Now, wait just a minute," he said, as the aisle began to fill with other passengers who tumbled out of their private compartments. "I didn't kill her."

"Yes, you did!"

Longarm wanted to slam the door in their faces and turn back the clock just a quarter hour as he realized he was in big, big trouble.

Chapter 6

The Marshal of Laramie and his two deputies got the drop on Longarm and there wasn't much he could do when they ordered him to raise his hands and marched him off the train toward their jail.

"Dammit, man, you're making a huge mistake," he told the burly marshal. "You need to immediately seal off this train and then we'll search for the murderer. Miss Durado's jewelry is missing and it was worth a fortune. When we find the jewelry, we'll know we have our killer."

"I think *you're* the killer," the marshal said, prodding Longarm sharply in the back with his gun barrel.

"I'm a United States deputy marshal!"

"I don't care who you are, mister. All that I know is that you've got the victim's blood on your hands. We've also got plenty of witnesses that said you were with the victim most of the evening. In fact, they say you had quite a time together in her little rolling love nest."

Marshal Ham Gunderson was a large block of bone and muscle, square-set and in his early thirties, with steely eyes that burned into Longarm like a brand. His two deputies were smaller and quiet as they held their guns trained on Longarm.

47

"Sure, Miss Durado and I were together," Longarm protested as they marched through Laramie. "But I came into her first-class compartment at the lady's invitation."

"I'll bet."

The way Gunderson said that left little doubt in Longarm's mind that the lawman didn't believe him. "And you've got scratches on your neck. Wanna explain those?"

Longarm reached up and touched the scratches. They weren't bleeding but they must have been bright red. "Miss Durado . . ." He couldn't say anything more, because a gentleman never talked about what he had done to or with a lady.

"Miss Durado, what?" Marshal Gunderson demanded.

"Never mind."

"You're under arrest for her murder and the theft of her jewels and money."

They were almost to the Laramie jail. Longarm's mind was racing, but he could see no way out of this mess. All he could do was to keep pleading with this blockhead to listen to the truth.

"Marshal Gunderson. My officer's badge is in my coat pocket. You'll see that I'm a duly appointed federal officer of the law. I am on my way to Nevada to work on a federal case. Now, we're wasting precious time! We must search every passenger on that train and we have to do it right now. He might already have sneaked off into your town."

"Shut up," Gunderson snarled as one of his deputies hurried ahead to unlock his office and then the jail cell. "You'll be brought before a judge next week and it'll be up to him to decide if you're innocent or guilty."

"Next week!" Longarm barked. "Are you crazy? By then the real killer will have disappeared and we may never find him. Marshal, we have to search that train now and . . ."

Longarm's protest ended in a grunt of pain as Gunderson drove a gun barrel into his spine and shoved him into the office with the warning, "Keep your hands over your head or I'll crack your skull. Search him, Charlie."

The deputy had a long, ferret-shaped face and dead-cold eyes. He looked like a gunfighter to Longarm and probably was. Charlie didn't waste any time finding Longarm's little derringer attached to his gold watch chain.

"Neat," Charlie said with clear admiration. "This guy makes a move like he's going to check the time on his watch and out comes that derringer. Real neat, Marshal Long."

"Yeah, ain't it, though," Gunderson said, taking Longarm's railroad watch and gold chain, along with the derringer. "Maybe I should have one of these made for myself."

"Or keep that one," Charlie said with a wink.

"Not a bad idea," Gunderson grunted. "Bill, get the jail cell opened up. We got ourselves a woman-killer."

Charlie next removed Longarm's badge and wallet. "Man's got almost two hundred dollars," he noted, licking his thin lips. "Sure a lot of money for an officer of the law to carry."

"Here, give it to me," the marshal said, taking the wallet and glancing at the cash. "How much money do you make each month, Marshal Long?"

"That's none of your damned business," Longarm snapped.

"Not *this* much," Gunderson said, pitching the wallet on his desk. "I'll bet most of it belonged to that rich woman you raped, robbed and then stabbed to death."

Longarm had the strongest impulse to attack this big fool. But that would have been suicidal, so he ground his teeth and then spat, "Maybe you'd better telegraph my boss at the Federal Building in Denver. He'll get you straightened out right away."

But Gunderson shook his head. "I don't like federal officers. They're all over-paid and under-worked. They come into our town and put on the dog, acting like they're better than we are. Like their shit don't stink. But they don't know squat and now I finally got me one that is a damned murderer."

"Marshal Gunderson, are you brain-damaged or completely insane?" Longarm demanded. "Because you're sounding like one or the other. And if we don't get on that train before it leaves and search every passenger, we've got no hope at all of finding Mona's killer."

"It'd be a waste of time, don't you agree, boys?"

The deputies, Charlie and Bill nodded their heads. Then Charlie said, "We got our murderer and that's for damn sure. There's blood on his hands and even scratches on his neck where the rich lady tried to fight him off. There are also witnesses who saw him with the knife in his hand."

"Hmmm," Gunderson said. "Before the train finishes taking on coal and water, you boys better get back on board and get written statements from those witnesses."

"But the train is leaving in about twenty minutes," Charlie said.

"Then get the hell out of here and get busy!" the marshal bellowed. "Get witnesses to say what needs to be said *before* that train rolls out of town, even if you have to hold them up a few minutes. Dammit, do you boys understand me?"

"Sure," Charlie said, as he grabbed Billy and they barreled out the door.

"Take off that fancy coat," Gunderson demanded, the gun still solid in his big fist. "And turn your pockets inside out. Maybe you got some other little tricks that Charlie missed. And remove your hat, gunbelt and boots. Do it all slow and easy and drop everything on the floor."

Longarm removed his coat first, then his hat and gunbelt. He was looking for a way . . . any way . . . to get out of this fix, because talking sense wasn't going to help his case. He'd have to stage his own jailbreak. Have to put

50

himself even farther behind the eight ball and mire himself even deeper in this quagmire.

But Longarm could see no other option. If that train pulled out, he'd never have a shot at finding Mona Durado's cold-blooded killer. Never in a hundred years. Even worse, he'd have no chance to prove his innocence. Marshal Gunderson was an imbecile, but that didn't change the fact that Longarm had been holding the murder knife when he'd been seen by that hysterical woman and other train passengers.

I have to get on that train before it leaves Laramie!

"Get those boots off and get into that cell."

Longarm knew that, once he was locked in the cell, any chance he had of catching his train was gone. So he tried to stall. "Gunderson, why are you being so pigheaded about this? Law officers ought to at least give each other the benefit of the doubt."

Gunderson sneered. "Like I said, I don't like you feds. I'll bet you make twice the money I make and you ain't nothin' but a fancy badge and a stuffed shirt."

"You're jealous."

"The hell you say! But once you're hanged, I'll be remembered as the man that brought a federal officer to justice. Maybe I'll be a little famous and get me a better job in a bigger and better town. Sure, I'll become the top dog in Cheyenne or even a warm place like Santa Fe, where the winters are warm and the women are all fast and easy."

"You're not only jealous and stupid, but you're driven by ambition."

"You talk too much. Take off them boots and get in that cell."

Longarm bent over and pulled off one boot, swaying and nearly falling. But he got the boot off and that's when he decided what he had to do.

"Other one," Gunderson grunted. "And hurry up."

Longarm cocked his left leg up and grabbed his boot. He staggered on purpose, then hopped forward as he tore the boot free and hurled it at Gunderson's round, beefy face.

The Laramie marshal's gun exploded, but his aim was deflected by the flying boot. The bullet actually tore through the boot and sent it flying past Longarm, who was already diving for Gunderson's knees.

They went down in a pile, Gunderson swearing and trying to get his gun pointed at Longarm so he could pull the trigger. But Longarm slammed the man's hand down on the rough plank floor and the gun exploded a second time, now shattering the glass in a rifle case. Failing to dislodge the gun from the crazy marshal's powerful hand, Longarm managed to sink his teeth in Gunderson's wrist.

"Ahh!" Gunderson bellowed, the gun finally dropping free.

Longarm snatched it up, took a sledgehammer-like blow to the side of his face and then swung with all his might. Gunderson's eyes rolled back in his head as his own pistol crashed against his rock-solid skull. When the local lawman still struggled, Longarm reared back and pistol-whipped him on the other side of his granite-thick head. This time, Gunderson slumped into unconsciousness.

Longarm felt as if he had been grappling with a gorilla—the man was that inhumanly strong. Staggering to his bare feet, Longarm grabbed Gunderson under the arms and dragged him toward the waiting jail cell.

"It's like dragging a damned mule," he muttered, finally getting Gunderson inside the cell, then slamming the door and locking it.

Longarm heard the train's whistle blast. That meant it was about to pull out of Laramie. He was running out of time.

As quickly as he could, Longarm pulled on his boots, coat and hat, then buckled his gun belt. He grabbed his wallet and badge and was heading for the door when he remembered that Gunderson had shoved the derringer and gold watch into his pocket.

"Damn!"

He raced back to the cell, rattled the keys and finally got the reluctant lock free. Throwing open the door, he strode into the cell and bent to retrieve his watch, chain and derringer.

"Ahh!" Gunderson cried, grabbing Longarm around the legs and pulling him down.

Longarm couldn't believe this man could still be conscious after taking two hard blows to the head by the barrel of his own six-gun. But here he was again, fighting for his very life in the cell.

"I'll save the hangman his fee!" Gunderson shouted, trying to get his hands on Longarm's throat and throttle him to death.

Longarm was a powerful man, but he was no match for Gunderson. That was obvious, and since he was fighting for his life, there were no holds barred. He bit, he tore and then he got a thumb in Gunderson's eye and tried to rip out the man's eyeball.

Gunderson screamed in agony and Longarm dug his thumb even deeper. When Gunderson released his own grip, Longarm slammed his knee into the marshal's crotch. Gunderson's good eye bulged in pain and his damaged eye rolled in its socket. Longarm jumped up and kicked the man in the jaw and Gunderson began to moan. Longarm retrieved his gold watch, chain and the hide-out derringer.

His legs felt like rubber and he was having trouble breathing because Gunderson had gotten his claws on his throat and nearly crushed it. Had the man gotten both hands on his neck, Longarm knew he would already be a dead man.

He staggered and grabbed the cell bars for support. Then he hauled himself outside the cell and relocked it.

Gunderson was in agony, still moaning. Longarm didn't know if he'd permanently blinded the man in one eye or not. It really didn't matter. Gunderson was an insane animal who had no business in the law profession.

"You should have been reasonable," he panted at the writhing man. "If you hadn't been so ambitious and pigheaded, we might already have the real killer in custody. But no, you wanted it to be a federal officer of the law. Damn your thick skull!"

Longarm staggered over to the lawman's desk and found his six-gun. He saw a pitcher of water on a washstand and went over to douse his face. He dried it, then looked at himself in the cracked and dirty office mirror.

"I look like I've been run over by a freight wagon," he muttered, holstering his gun as he headed for the door, still hearing Gunderson's heavy moans from the cell.

He knew that he stood a very good chance of running into Gunderson's deputies, Bill and Charlie. In that case, he'd just have to figure out a way to get the drop on them and then get on the train as it was pulling out of Laramie.

And what would he say to the people on the train who were so sure that he had murdered Miss Durado? He'd think of something.

Damn his bad luck and damn the man who had killed that lovely lady. If the killer was still on the train, somehow, some way, Longarm would find the murdering sonofabitch.

Chapter 7

Longarm reached the train just as it was pulling out of the
Laramie station and he was running after it when shots
rang out across the loading platform. Longarm saw a bullet
dig splinters out of the train's caboose and he whirled
around just in time to see Bill and Charlie sprinting after
him with guns blazing.

He didn't want to return fire. The two deputies were just
doing their jobs, and besides, Longarm had a feeling they
weren't very bright.

So with his lungs burning and his heart pumping, Longarm leapt up on the back of the caboose and rolled up tight
against the closed door, while bullets sent splinters flying
over his head. In a minute, perhaps less, the train had out-
distanced the deputies and the firing had ceased.

One of the porters opened the rear door of the caboose,
stared at Longarm and then tried to slam the door shut
again. Longarm managed to get his foot into the opening
and keep it from closing, then he forced the door open and
rolled inside.

The porter wasn't armed and he was scared. "Don't
shoot me!"

Longarm was too winded to even reply for several moments. "Why in the devil would I *shoot* you?"

But the fool was too frightened to hear. "I ain't got any money. There ain't no reason to kill me, Marshal. I got a wife and five kids. Don't kill me. Please!"

Longarm was too disgusted to reply. With his breath returning and his heart no longer pounding in his chest, he hauled himself erect and gazed out through the open doorway at the deputies who were standing in the middle of the track, slowly fading into the distance.

"What a damned, stupid mess this is," he swore to himself. Then, turning to the porter, he said, "Where is the next stop?"

"Rawlins."

"Does the train take on water and coal there?"

"No, sir."

Longarm guessed that was about eighty-five miles away. "Is a telegraph operator there at the Rawlins station?"

"Yes, sir."

"Where does the train take on water and coal again?"

"We'll need to take it on at Rock Springs."

"How far are we from Rock Springs right now?"

"About two hundred miles." The porter gulped.

Longarm pulled out his gold watch. "That gives me roughly five hours. Right?"

"Yes, sir. It is, if you don't kill me."

The porter was a homely man in his forties. He was bald with bat ears and an Adam's apple that bobbed up and down his turkey neck when he spoke. The man could not have weighed a 120 pounds soaking wet and he was so frightened of Longarm that his knees were knocking.

"Relax," Longarm said, feeling guilty about putting such a scare into this frail and timid fellow. It was hard to imagine the little runt had fathered five children. "What's your name?"

"Homer Q. Holbrook, sir. I got five kids to support and . . ."

"Yeah, I know," Longarm said. "You already told me."

"If you kill me, my kids will go hungry and my wife will never forgive you. She'll put a curse on your name, Marshal Long."

"Well," Longarm said, "that won't be necessary because I have no intention of orphaning your kids, if you do as I ask."

"Whatever you say, I'll do it!" the man cried, clasping his bony hands together in a pathetic act of supplication. "Just tell me what you need and it's as good as done."

"Sit down and let's talk," Longarm ordered, taking a seat across from the trembling porter. "What are you doing back here in the caboose?"

"I was going to leave when the shooting started. But the front door jammed and the harder I pulled the tighter she stuck."

"You know about the death of Miss Durado?"

He swallowed hard. "Yes, sir."

"Well," Longarm said wearily, "I *didn't* kill her. I'm a federal officer of the law. Want to see my badge?"

"No, sir. I believe you."

"Do you believe that I am innocent of Miss Durado's murder?"

"Sure, if that's what you want me to believe."

Longarm doubted he could trust Homer, but there was little choice. Given that everyone on the train would recognize him if he headed for the front cars to investigate the murder and discover the culprit, he first needed some assistance.

"What I need is for you to tell me who was in the first-class coach, and if any of those people were single men. Also, I want to know if they are still on the train or if they departed at Laramie. Can you do that?"

"I can do it easy. I'll just go down the first-class passenger list. And I already know most of it."

"Good," Longarm told the man. "I wasn't gone but about ten or fifteen minutes to the coach car when the murder took place. So whoever did it must have been either in the first-class or the next car back. And I think we can eliminate the next car back as well as those men who were traveling with their wives. Also, any man that you think is too feeble to do such a murder. Miss Durado was a strong young woman and she wouldn't have been easy to kill. But someone did and it wasn't me."

"No, sir," Homer Holbrook said, shaking his head back and forth.

"I want you to go now and bring me back names and descriptions of the likely killers. Also what compartment they are in. If you do that, you'll be fine. If you cross me up and tell anyone that I'm back here waiting for your report, I will hunt you down and slice your big ears off. Got it?"

"Yes, sir!"

"Don't double-cross me, Homer. Your kids and your wife are depending on you to do as you promised."

"I won't fail you."

"I hope not, for your own sake," Longarm told the shaking man. "Now go, and don't keep me waiting. I have to find the real murderer before we reach Rock Springs."

Homer again tried to pry open the jammed door, but failed. Longarm eased the weakling aside and wrenched the door open. "They ought to fix this damned thing," he said as Homer ducked under his arm and shot out of the caboose like a rabbit.

Longarm was famished, and when he spied a metal lunch pail, he pounced upon it without hesitation. The pail had Homer's name neatly printed on the outside. Inside, Longarm found a cheese sandwich on thin, hard bread, a shriveled old apple and a few dried nuts.

"No wonder the poor guy is so skinny," he muttered as

he wolfed down the man's lunch. "I'd be as skinny as a rail if this was the best I got to eat every day. But I'll bet Homer's wife is as big as a barn."

Homer was back in less than twenty minutes. Looking flushed, excited and nervous, he produced the passenger list. "I sneaked it out of the conductor's cubbyhole," he confessed. "And I looked up the gentlemen passengers that were traveling alone. There are only three."

"Tell me their names, approximate ages and what they look like."

He wiped sweat from his brow. "Do you mind if I sit down and rest? Running all the way up through the train sure took the starch out of me, and my heart ain't the best, you know."

The man did look pale.

"Sure, sit down."

"I'm real hungry and . . . darn it, you ate my lunch!"

The man looked stricken. "It wasn't much of a lunch," Longarm said, feeling a twinge of guilt. He dug into his pocket and found a silver dollar. Here, when this is over, go to the dining car and buy yourself something better to eat."

"A dollar won't buy hardly anything in our dining car. The prices they charge are higher than a camel's back."

Longarm reluctantly gave the porter another dollar. "Now tell me about our murder suspects."

"All right," the porter began, sitting hunched over and wringing his hands. "The first one is Mr. Jason Atherton. He's about fifty years old. Fat man with a walrus mustache. He farts constantly and I don't think he's the one that killed Miss Durado."

"Why not?"

"Because he travels frequently on this train and we've never had a killing before. Besides, he is so fat that he has trouble getting in and out of his compartment. He's very demanding and a lot of trouble. I always hate to see him on board."

"What does he do for a living?"

"He sells jewelry. Most of it is cheap but he has a few quality pieces."

"Miss Durado had some wonderful jade jewelry," Longarm said. "So the man is a good suspect."

Homer still looked unconvinced. "Well, I sure don't think so. He brings a basket of food with him and is always eating. He's kind of fussy and I just don't think he's the one."

"Who's next?"

"Mr. C. J. Taylor from Rock Springs. He's a rancher, I believe. Large man in his early thirties. He walks with a bad limp so he probably didn't do it, either. Oh, and he's missing the thumb on his left hand. He really doesn't seem like someone who would kill a woman."

"He might have," Longarm said. "What's he like?"

"Nice enough man and very quiet. He's a widower and once told me he owns about a thousand head of cattle."

"Does he ride this train often?"

"About twice a year."

Longarm doubted that C. J. was his man. Cowboys and ranchers were hardworking people and not the kind to use a knife on an enemy. "Who is the third man?"

The porter smiled. "Dr. Mark Payne, but he wouldn't hurt a fly. He's a California doctor and *very* religious. You rarely see Dr. Payne when he isn't reading either the Holy Bible or his scientific journals. He also smokes a pipe with a very aromatic brand of expensive tobacco."

"How old is the doctor?"

"About my age."

"And that would be?"

"Forty-three, Marshal Long. Forty-four next January. I was born on . . ."

"Is Dr. Payne a big or small man?" Longarm interrupted.

"Average size. The doctor is a very snappy dresser. He

cuts a handsome and refined figure. But he would never kill anyone."

"How do you know that for sure?"

"The Hippocratic oath," Homer explained. "All doctors have to take it and promise to preserve life."

"Does the man carry a medical kit?"

Homer frowned. "No, come to think of it, he does not. I'm sure he is quite a wealthy gentleman. My guess is that Dr. Payne is already retired, lucky stiff. I'll be working on this train until I'm ready for the bone yard. I started on this train shoveling coal way back in . . ."

"Maybe," Longarm suggested, "Dr. Payne isn't really a *medical* doctor. Some academic professors call themselves doctors. He might be a doctor specializing in geology or literature."

"I'm quite sure he is a medical doctor," Homer insisted.

"Did you see any of these three men with Miss Durado before she was murdered?"

"No."

"Are their compartments near hers?"

"Oh, yes. All three."

"If you had to choose among the trio, which would you think is most likely the murderer?"

"Hmmm. Actually, I don't think any of them is capable of murder. Are you sure that the killer is in first class?" Homer asked. "Because back in coach, there are a lot of unsavory loners."

"Well," Longarm said, "they would have had to pass me on the way up to Miss Durado's compartment and no one from coach did that. And furthermore, it is unlikely that they would have even met the lady."

"You're in coach and *you* met her," Homer said, then realized his mistake and gulped loudly. "Not that it means anything, Marshal."

Longarm hardly heard the porter and mused aloud.

"Somehow, I must find a way to acquaint myself with those three primary suspects."

"How are you going to do that? They all think you're back in Laramie under arrest for murder. So if they saw you on the train, they and everyone else would go into a complete panic. Actually, I'm pretty nervous around you myself."

"You have an excellent point." Longarm thought hard, then said, "What do you do when we reach Rawlins?"

"You mean during the stop?"

"That's right."

"Load and unload baggage, supplies, mail and passengers," Homer told him. "We usually aren't in Rawlins more than thirty or forty minutes."

"Could you get into town and buy me a set of clothes and a derby hat, perhaps? And a wig, if you could find one?"

"A *wig*?"

"Yes. Theatrical houses have them for their thespians."

"There are no theatrical houses in Rawlins, Marshal. It's just a rough railroad town."

"Then new clothes will have to do," Longarm said. "And I'll . . . dammit, shave off my mustache and . . . and get some charcoal that I can use to darken my eyebrows. That should do it. Oh, and I'll need you to escort me into Miss Durado's vacated compartment for the trip between Rawlins and Rock Springs. Yes, that ought to do it."

"But . . ."

Longarm counted out fifty dollars and gave it to Homer. He hated to spend the money but there was little choice. If he simply appeared as himself, it would be very near impossible to avoid creating panic in first class, not to mention getting any kind of an interview with the three single men who were now the prime suspects. So he had to affect a new identity.

"I will be Mr. William Vail," he said, assuming his boss's name. "I'm a traveling salesman."

"What do you sell?"

Longarm smiled. "Hmmm. You're right. I'd better think of something. Oh, I'll sell land. Yes, that is the thing. I'll be a land salesman on my way to Reno."

The porter eyed him skeptically. "I'm not sure this will work, Marshal Long."

"If it doesn't, then I'll arrest all three, escort them back here to the caboose and get the truth out of them one way or the other. Mona's jewelry is missing and one of them has to have it either on his person or hidden in his compartment. I'll figure out a way."

Homer studied the fifty dollars. "Marshal, are you sure that you want to do this?"

"I'm sure," Longarm told him. "Now get what I need and hurry back here after you do my shopping in Rawlins."

"Can I keep what I don't spend? I mean, you ate my *lunch* and I'm really sticking my neck out for you."

"Fine," Longarm agreed. "But I'm supposed to be a successful real-estate salesperson so don't buy me shabby clothes."

"I won't," Homer promised.

Longarm watched the little man leave the caboose. He sure wished that he had more faith in Homer and in the kind of disguise the porter would buy.

Chapter 8

"Here," Homer said, looking completely out of sorts as he handed Longarm a package wrapped in brown paper. "I got you a black suit, derby hat, black shoes and tie, along with a starched white shirt. I didn't know your size so I got the biggest they had, and it wasn't cheap."

"How much?"

"Sixty-three dollars."

Longarm scowled. "That's considerably more than I either expected or wanted to pay."

"Yeah, I know, but that's what the price was so you owe me thirteen dollars."

Longarm knew the man didn't have a receipt so rather than argue the sum, he just paid it. "This better be quality stuff," he growled as he opened the package.

Longarm's eyes bugged. "This suit is big enough to clothe a damn elephant! Why, I'd have to weigh three hundred pounds for it to fit!"

"Yeah," Homer snapped, "but at least it's long enough in the sleeves and pants."

Longarm was furious. He tried on the hat, and of course, it was a half size too small. Seething, he tried the shoes and was greatly relieved to see that they, at least, fit.

"I'm going to look like a damned clown," he groused as he tried to think of how he could pin up the pants and wear the coat so he didn't look completely ridiculous.

"Did you get any charcoal?"

"Sure."

Longarm saw that it was just a hunk but it would serve to darken his eyebrows. "Now I need you to go to the coach car and get my razor, strop and other personal belongings."

"I *do* have a job on this train," Homer complained. "And if I keep running errands for you I'll probably get fired."

"Just go get my things, then I'll do the rest."

Homer wasn't happy. "I haven't even had something to eat since early this morning. No time."

"Get my things," Longarm ordered, "then eat."

Homer left the caboose grousing and whining.

When the train pulled into Rawlins, Longarm was ready in his new disguise although he'd had to dry shave in the caboose and his face was cut and scraped red. He knew he looked awful and felt ridiculous. The only saving grace was that there was no mirror available in the caboose or he probably would have given up the whole idea of a false identity. But he'd paid out over sixty dollars and he was determined to get into Mona's now-vacated compartment so that he could be near the three murder suspects. What he would actually do about them he still had no idea.

So he got the razor nicks to stop bleeding, cinched up his way-oversized pants so they would not fall to his feet, causing him untold embarrassment, then crammed the too-small derby down on his head and stepped off the train for its brief stop in Rawlins.

Most of the passengers chose the opportunity to really stretch their legs and get a breath of fresh air, which gave Longarm a chance to get a clear view of his three primary suspects.

Because of his immense girth, it was easy to recognize Jason Atherton. The man was a whale and made quite a show of marching up and down the Rawlins train depot windmilling his huge arms and puffing like the nearby locomotive. He was about six feet tall and had deep-set little eyes that flitted about constantly. Longarm stayed far enough away from the man so that he didn't have to endure his constant expelling of noxious gas, but he heard Atherton even over the chuff-chuffing of the nearby locomotive.

"Homer is probably right. He's too big to have slipped into Mona's small compartment and stabbed her. Yet he does move well despite his size, so I shouldn't eliminate Mr. Atherton as a suspect. And he is a man who would recognize the great value of Mona's jewelry."

Longarm felt very self-conscious as he stood in the shadows, watching the passengers talk and get a little vigorous exercise. Then he spotted Dr. Mark Payne. The man was handsome and cultured. He stood aloof from the other passengers and tended to his pipe. The breeze was blowing a bit and Longarm caught the fragrance of the man's expensive pipe tobacco. A large diamond ring glittered on his hand and his tailored, gray pin-striped suit was perfectly fitted to his slender, graceful figure.

He was a dandy. But could he also be a murderer? Longarm watched the doctor for several minutes, trying to judge him, but finally gave up. Dr. Payne was impossible to read. On the one hand, he looked to be a sophisticate; on the other he might be a fraud, even a gigolo who had conned his way into Mona's compartment the moment Longarm had disappeared and then wasted no time in killing her for her jewelry. He would be, Longarm suspected, very smooth and persuasive. It was also likely that he had conversed previously with Miss Durado.

"Definitely a prime suspect," Longarm said to himself.

The final suspect that the porter had identified as a single male traveling alone in the first-class coach was the rancher, C. J. Taylor. He was a tall, muscular fellow who walked with a pronounced limp that should have required a cane. But Taylor was a rugged outdoorsman, with sun-weathered brown skin and broad shoulders. And yes, he was missing the thumb on his left hand. Had this been the East, Longarm would have assumed that the missing thumb had been the result of the Civil War. But since this was the West, the loss was more likely to have been the result of a fight or a bad dally with a rope around the saddle horn. Lots of cowboys lost digits that way, roping horses and cattle.

Despite his limp, C. J. Taylor cut an impressive figure. At six-four and well over two-hundred pounds, he caused men to step aside as he limped up and down the railroad platform, eyes missing little or nothing. Once, they stopped on Longarm and studied him for a penetrating instant. Longarm offered the rancher a slight smile, but it wasn't returned. C. J. Taylor had a crooked nose and a scar on his right cheek. And although he wasn't visibly wearing a sidearm, there was little doubt in Longarm's mind that the rancher had a hide-out gun and probably a bowie knife hidden on his body.

For ten minutes, all three suspects were in Longarm's view and he studied them carefully, trying to read something out of their mannerisms and movements. In the end, as the train whistle blew announcing to the passengers that the train was preparing to leave Rawlins, Longarm decided that the most likely killer was Dr. Mark Payne, followed by the fat man, Jason Atherton, and then the rancher, C. J. Taylor.

"I'll interview them in that order," he said to himself, as he waited until the last passenger was on board and then hurried across the depot and jumped onto the train. "And, if none of the three are Mona's killer, then I'll work my way back on the train to the coach car. If I must, I'll search every pocket, every suitcase and even every purse until I find that jade jewelry and the killer."

With that at least settled in his mind, Longarm met the porter, Homer Holbrook, in the aisle of first class and the nervous little man hurried him into Mona Durado's vacated first-class compartment.

Chapter 9

Longarm had decided he would sneak into each man's compartment while they were dining. Since their spaces were cramped, he was certain that he could do all three searches in less than fifteen minutes. And, if that turned up nothing, he would corner each suspect and search his person.

An hour out of Rawlins, the conductor came down the aisle calling, "Dinner is being served in the dining car. Dinner is being served in the dining car."

Longarm applied the charcoal to his eyebrows. Since his luxuriant handlebar mustache was now shaved away, the skin on his upper lip was unnaturally pale, so he tried to use just a trace of charcoal there, too. But it looked like he'd been nibbling on dirt, so he wiped that away. Inspecting himself in the small mirror, he knew that he appeared so comical he'd have trouble fooling a blind man.

"The hell with it," he growled, tossing the too-small derby hat aside as he waited impatiently for the first-class passengers to make their way past his cramped compartment to the dining car.

He gave them plenty of time, then he ducked his head out into the aisle. Seeing no one, he went to Dr. Payne's compartment and eased his way inside. It was, like the man himself, neat and tidy. Dr. Payne traveled light, with the exception of his books and scientific journals. Longarm glanced at a Bible, then at the journals and saw that they related to archaeology. It confirmed his early hunch that Payne wasn't a medical doctor.

Longarm had searched hundreds of rooms and people for damning evidence and had perfected the art of leaving no trace of his presence. It took him less than five minutes to search the overhead luggage and bedding compartment, then the bed itself and the luggage. During that time, he did find a box of bullets and a small handgun. Otherwise, he discovered nothing of importance and certainly no stolen jewelry.

On to the fat man's compartment. As fastidious as Dr. Payne's first-class compartment had been, Mr. Atherton's was messy. The man had obviously secreted great quantities of cookies, crackers, cheese and other foodstuff onto the train, hidden in his luggage. The little compartment could have fed a thousand mice for six months; it was that littered with scraps, wrappings and crumbs.

Atherton had no reading material and his baggage was expensive but held little of value. It mostly contained the remaining food that the man thought necessary to supplement what he could devour in the railroad's expensive dining car. Longarm found no gun, knife or other weapon, but he did find some papers relating to jewelry sales and orders. He could tell by the stationery that Mr. Atherton lived and worked out of Sacramento, California.

"This guy has got to be the one," Longarm said, riffling through the man's clothing and other disorganized belongings. "But where is Miss Durado's jewelry? Where's my evidence?"

Frustrated, he completed his search for the second time, then threw up his hands in frustration. He had found nothing but a glutton's larder. "Maybe the man has all of Miss

Durado's jewels on his person. As big as he is, it would be easy enough to hide them in his pockets."

Longarm hurried over to the rancher's private compartment. C. J. Taylor's space was neither cluttered nor ordered and there was a saddle, horse blanket and bridle stuffed in one corner and a Winchester rifle propped up against the wall. Longarm began without much hope of finding anything. But then he discovered something *very* interesting.

A letter from a bank in Cheyenne. A letter that demanded six thousand dollars on an overdue mortgage. Longarm scanned the letter and it indicated that it was the last of several demands for payment. Payment which, if not made immediately, would result in an imminent foreclosure on Taylor's cattle ranch located outside of Rock Springs.

"Means and motive," Longarm said. "But no evidence, yet."

He replaced the letter in its official envelope, made sure that everything was as he had found it and then turned to leave, when the big rancher stepped into the doorway with a gun in his fist.

"Find anything interesting?" Taylor asked in a voice that was chilling despite its casualness.

"Oh," Longarm said, trying to fake surprise and confusion. "I must have stumbled into the wrong compartment and was just leaving. I'm sorry."

"Sure you did, Marshal Long," the rancher said, viciously swinging the barrel of the gun upward toward Longarm's face.

Longarm managed to throw his forearm up fast enough to deflect the blow . . . but only partially. The gun barrel slammed against his jaw. Longarm staggered and fell backward, off balance. Taylor closed the door behind him and drew a knife from his belt.

"Marshal, you'd have been better off takin' your chances in Laramie," the big man growled.

Longarm was armed and he fumbled for his derringer, but the oversized coat and pants he was wearing hampered his efforts. He abandoned the effort when Taylor lunged at him with the knife. Longarm grabbed the man's wrist and twisted with all his strength. The long-bladed knife slashed downward, just missing his throat as it buried its steel into the seat's upholstery. The rancher was on top of Longarm and he drew back his knife and started pushing it downward for a killing thrust.

The contest was brute strength against brute strength. Two big and powerful men locked in deadly combat. Unfortunately, Longarm was on the bottom as the blade inched down toward his chest until its tip met the silver-dollar-sized garnet pendant that Lilly had given him and which was hidden under his shirt.

"What the hell!" the rancher cried in frustration.

Longarm seized that moment of confusion to save his life as he twisted violently, throwing the rancher aside. Then he buried his teeth in Taylor's wrist. The killer's fingers spasmed, then released the knife. Longarm rolled hard, tore his derringer free and pressed it into Taylor's gut, hissing, "Freeze or I'll pull the trigger!"

The desperate rancher had no intention of freezing. He tried to push Longarm's gun aside and twist it back on his enemy. He head-butted Longarm, who pulled the derringer's trigger, causing a muffled explosion. C. J. Taylor's eyes grew wide, filling with shock and hatred a moment before he cursed and died.

Longarm was covered with blood and his senses were reeling from the head-butt he'd just received. He rolled Taylor aside and climbed to his feet, grabbing at the closed-in walls for support, while he tried to clear his mind. His fingers absently caressed the garnet pendant, and Longarm offered a silent but heartfelt thanks to Miss Lilly Hutton.

Apparently, the derringer's explosion had been muffled

by their bodies and the hammering of wheels on iron rails. No one came rushing down the aisle and so after a few minutes Longarm tore off his bloody, ill-fitting suit and searched the dead rancher's person.

Nothing!

Longarm groaned. Where were Miss Durado's expensive jewels!

He was still leaning against the walls of the small compartment when a knock sounded on the door.

"C. J.?"

"In here."

The door opened and there stood the fat man, with a smile on his round face now melting like butter in the blazing sun.

Longarm's hand shot out and he grabbed Jason Atherton and somehow managed to pull him through the narrow doorway and into the compartment. He slammed the door behind them. Atherton had seen the blood and his dead accomplice. He squealed in rage and fear, and tried to overpower Longarm with his size and weight. Longarm gave the man no chance at all. He brought a knee up into Atherton's testicles and the jewelry salesman squealed again.

Longarm didn't have much in the way of fighting space, but he made the best of it. Three vicious uppercuts into that immense belly and an overhead right-cross to the face came in rapid succession. Atherton slumped to the floor, helpless and wedged between the seats and wall.

"Which pocket?" Longarm demanded.

Atherton's nose was broken and he was whimpering.

"Which damned pocket!" Longarm shouted. "Tell me or I'll kick your bloody face in!"

Atherton sobbed, "OK! OK!"

And then, his fat hand disappeared into his coat pocket and emerged with Miss Durado's stolen jewelry.

Longarm snatched it from the man. "*You* murdered her."

"No, C. J. did!" Atherton cried, eyes jumping to the

rancher's body. "I swear that it was C.J.'s idea all the way. He was going to lose his Wyoming cattle ranch. I simply bought Miss Durado's jewels from him. I didn't have anything to do with murdering that poor woman."

"Sure you did," Longarm said, without a shred of pity. "You agreed to buy them after C.J. knifed Miss Durado to death. That makes you an accomplice to murder. If you hang, they'll use a chain to hold your weight; if you go to prison, you'll *never* be set free."

"Please!" the fat man sobbed. "I won't survive in prison. They won't feed me enough and the other prisoners will . . . rape me."

Longarm stared at the jewels in his fist. He didn't bother telling Jason Atherton that he would get in prison exactly what he deserved.

"Marshal Pickens," Longarm said, reading the man's name on his desk plaque, "I have a new tenant for you. This is Jason Atherton and he's an accomplice to murder."

Pickens had been reading the local newspaper. He was a tall, thin drink of water in his early sixties, with a droopy gray mustache stained yellow from chewing tobacco. He wore a floppy gray Stetson, also stained with tobacco, and a pair of patched brown britches and a yellow shirt that had seen better days. Longarm had always thought that a town marshal ought to take pride in his appearance because, if he looked unkempt and rumpled, then he would get little respect. However, it was obvious that Marshal Pickens did not share that view.

"I already used up my budget for this month," the marshal said without taking his feet off his desk. "I ain't got any money to feed a hog-fat prisoner."

"Then *don't* feed him," Longarm said, anxious to return to the train. "I'm guessing Atherton will do just fine on bread and water for a few months."

Atherton whimpered piteously.

Pickens finally dropped his feet from the desk and studied Longarm. "You sure are dressed funny," he drawled. "Those clothes are twice your size. Have you been real sick?"

"Marshal, it's a long story."

"You need to put some meat on your bones, 'cause your pants are about to fall off."

"These clothes were my disguise on the train." Longarm did not see what his dress had to do with anything, so he changed the subject. "I see that you already have two prisoners in your jail."

"Yep, and there ain't room for a third. At least not one that big."

"Then chain Atherton to the damn cell," Longarm snapped, running out of patience with this contrary lawman. "I don't have time to figure it out for you. Give me a paper and pencil and I'll fill out the details of the railroad murder and then sign Atherton over to you for trial."

"Nope," Pickens said, his jaw tightening, "I ain't takin' your prisoner 'cause I don't have the money to feed or care for him. Now, I strongly suggest that you get back on that westbound train with your prisoner. We got a full house here in Rock Springs and I'm already over my budget this month."

Longarm couldn't believe what he was hearing. "Marshal Pickens, I'm a federal officer of the law. A United States deputy marshal out of Denver, and I'm telling you that this man took stolen jewelry from a woman who was murdered here in Wyoming."

"Take him back to Rawlins," Pickens said. "He ain't goin' in my jail and I won't tell you that again!"

Longarm was astounded. "What the hell kind of a half-assed marshal are you?" he roared. "A woman was murdered on the train. I shot the murderer and this man was his accomplice. Now, how can I make you understand that you are *required* to take this man as your prisoner?"

"I ain't required to do jack-shit."

Longarm had a irresistible urge to jump forward, grab Pickens by the neck and throttle him like a stewing chicken. But he knew that would not solve any problems, so he fought off his anger and managed to say, "All right, Pickens. If that is the way you feel, then I'll make other arrangements for my prisoner."

Pickens sneered and snapped his suspenders in triumph. "I figured you would, Mr. Federal Officer."

Longarm grabbed Atherton and shoved him out the door.

"What are you going to do with me now?" the fat man asked.

"I haven't decided yet."

"Just let me go," Atherton begged. "C. J. said he was going to steal that poor woman's jewelry. He never said anything about murdering her."

"You had a chance to come forward," Longarm said. "You could have set the record straight and saved me from being arrested and tossed in jail while the train was in Rawlins. But you kept quiet."

"C. J. would have killed me, too, if I'd so much as peeped as to what he'd done. Can't you understand that?"

Longarm shoved the fat man toward the train. He could hear the conductor yelling for everyone to get on board. "Run!" he shouted, pushing the fat man into a stumbling rush. "If we miss that train, I swear I'll kill you here and now."

Atherton must have believed Longarm because he did his best to run, but it was pitiful. The man was puffing like the locomotive and wheezing like a sick draft horse by the time they hauled themselves on board.

"Oh, my! Oh, my!" the fat man cried, falling in the aisle and grabbing his chest. "I think my heart is giving out on me and I'm going to die!"

Longarm had to admit that Atherton did look real pasty.

He knelt beside the gasping man and grabbed his pulse. It was hammering like crazy and Atherton was covered with a cold sweat.

"Breathe deep!" Longarm ordered. "Slow down and breathe deep."

But the fat man was beginning to quiver. He grabbed his chest and tried to speak.

"What's wrong with him!" the conductor shouted.

"He's having a heart failure," Longarm said. "I've seen it before. Is there a doctor on this train?"

"Yes."

"Then hurry up and get him," Longarm ordered.

The conductor disappeared. Longarm didn't know what he could do to help Jason Atherton. He wished he hadn't pushed the fat man so hard, but he'd been angry at Marshal Pickens and in a hurry to catch the train. Still, there would have been another train coming along in a few days.

"I'm sorry," Longarm told the dying fat man, who was gasping and flailing around. "I didn't mean for this to happen."

But Atherton couldn't reply. Instead, he shuddered, then his enormous body heaved a monstrous sigh and was still.

"Shit!" Longarm swore, in anger, knowing that the man had probably been telling the truth about his role in Miss Durado's murder. For despite his size, Atherton had been a weakling and a coward. He'd also been dishonest. Still, those shortcomings didn't deserve the kind of death that Longarm had precipitated.

"Step aside!" the doctor ordered, rushing up to them.

"Doc, I'm afraid the man is already gone," Longarm said as the train gathered speed. "There isn't anything you could have done."

The doctor studied the body. "A man that big, he would have died an early death. It was just a matter of when and where. Who was he?"

"A jewelry salesman. He wasn't much of a man, Doc."

"Well, what are you going to do with his body, now that the train is moving?"

Longarm shrugged and turned to the conductor. "He's your passenger. You figure it out."

The conductor wasn't happy. "Well, dammit, we sure as the devil can't drag a body that size through the train all the way back to the mail car!"

"And you can't just shove him out onto the tracks," the doctor said. "My advice is just to leave the corpse where it lies and cover him with a sheet of canvas. Then, at the next town, we can get him to a cemetery."

Longarm thought that was a reasonable solution, so he left the two to work out the details. He needed something to eat and something strong to drink. All in all, this had been one of the worst train journeys he'd ever experienced. And he sure as hell hoped it didn't portend what was waiting for him in Nevada.

Chapter 10

Longarm kept to himself during the rest of the journey west to Elko, Nevada. He slept, rested and insisted on staying in Miss Durado's first-class compartment. The railroad people didn't like that, but since they had no other passengers who had paid to take the space, he was allowed to remain there. Also, given the deaths that had occurred on the journey, everyone connected with the train just wanted him out of sight and out of mind.

During the time that the train passed the Great Salt Lake he was filled with a sadness at Miss Durado's loss. At some point, he would need to write a letter to her relatives in California, explaining her death. He also needed to make sure that her expensive jewelry and belongings made their way to her home.

Many times as the train crawled across Utah, he fingered the garnet pendant that Miss Lilly Hutton had given him as a talisman. He vividly remembered how C. J. Taylor had gotten the better of him in this very compartment and would have driven his knife into his heart had it not been for the garnet pendant. She had promised Longarm it would bring him back home to her safely, and he thought perhaps it did have some special protective power. Whether that was true or not, he was certainly going to wear the garnet the rest of this assignment and tell Lilly about how it had saved his life.

He had promised to telegraph Miss Hutton when he reached Elko and he would keep that promise. And, he couldn't help but wonder if he should consider marrying Lilly. There were many reasons for doing so. She was beautiful, a tiger in bed despite her total lack of experience, and most importantly she loved him deeply. Oh, yes, and there was also the fact that her father was rich and influential in Colorado. This, unfortunately, might very well prove to be more trouble than it was a benefit. To Longarm's way of thinking, a rich father-in-law could be easily become a royal pain in the ass.

"But I'll telegraph Lilly as soon as I step off the train in Elko," he mused out loud to himself. "It's the least I can do, given that I took her virginity and her garnet stone saved my life. I suppose I love her, but I love them all. However, maybe I will wind up marrying the girl. I'll just have to give it more thought. If this assignment turns out to be especially bad, I might be ready to make some major changes in my life."

When the train rolled into Elko, Nevada, Longarm was more than ready to disembark. He still didn't exactly understand what he was doing here, but he had also promised to send his boss a telegram. He found the telegraph office where they were usually located, right near the railroad tracks, and sent a message to Billy Vail, which was brief and to the point.

Billy:

I had some trouble on the way out here to Nevada. A woman's murder took place on the train and I had to kill the murderer. His accomplice checked out with a weak heart. It's all very complicated and cost me

82

*most of my government travel money. So please wire
another hundred and any new information as to why
I'm here.*

                                                    Custis

The telegraph operator frowned. "Is that all?"

"It's enough. How much do I owe you?"

He squinted down at the brief message and counted the words. "One dollar and sixty cents."

"OK," Longarm said, taking up the pencil and fresh sheet of paper. "I got another telegram I want to send. This one is for Miss Lilly Hutton." He scribbled:

Dear Lilly,

*I got here OK and hope to wrap up in two weeks
or less. It was a bad trip but your garnet pendant really saved my bacon. I miss you and hope you are in
good spirits and health.*

                                                    Custis

The telegraph operator was a man in his mid-twenties, owlish looking, with thick glasses. "Is that all?"

"It'll do," Longarm said.

"Excuse me," the man said, "But what do you mean, 'your garnet pendant saved my bacon'?"

"She'll understand, but it isn't important that you do. So how much for the second telegram?"

The telegraph operator figured it out while shaking his head. Clearly, he was the nosy type, and his curiosity was getting the best of him. "Are you sure that she will understand about the garnet thing?"

"Yep."

"All right. Both telegrams will cost you two dollars and a dime."

Longarm gave the man three silver dollars. "I'll be staying at the Elko Hotel. You can keep the change, so long as you notify me the minute I get any return telegrams. Especially the one from my boss authorizing me more money."

"You must be a federal officer."

"I am," Longarm replied. "Name is Deputy Marshal Custis Long. I've come here to see about the train robbery and the theft of government bonds. I also understand there have been several unsolved murders, as well as troubles with the Indians."

"That's right. So where is the United States Army?" The telegraph operator forced a weak smile. "No disrespect intended, Marshal Long, but all this trouble we have in Elko is sure going to take more than you to fix."

"We'll see," he told the man. "Just make sure that I get any incoming telegrams and that they stay private. I won't have you spreading my damned business around town for gossip."

The young man blinked, cleared his throat and managed to appear very offended. "Why, of course! All business that comes in and out of this telegraph office is strictly confidential."

Longarm had had enough bad experiences with telegraph offices to know that wasn't usually the case. So, in addition to the tip, he gave the man a clear warning. "That's good to know. However, if I find out anyone but you and me learns of my official communications, I'll arrest you for a federal offense that will send you straight to a federal prison. Understood?"

The man paled and managed to stammer, "You don't need to threaten me, Marshal Long."

"Good. Now who is your local marshal?"

"His name is Orvis Nestor. But I'm afraid that you won't find him in his office today."

"Why not?"

"This is Wednesday. He goes rabbit hunting on Wednesday."

Longarm was not sure that he had heard correctly. "Did you say your town marshal is taking off the day to go rabbit hunting?"

"That's right. And Sunday is the Sabbath so he isn't in and Saturday Orvis is generally fishing all day for catfish in the Humboldt River, if the weather permits."

Longarm scowled. "Does Marshal Orvis Nestor have a deputy?"

"Yes. His name is Deputy Don Coon. But Coon goes rabbit hunting with Marshal Nestor, so that's why the office will be locked up today."

"And I suppose he and the marshal also are gone on Saturday fishing?"

"Yep. They're tighter than ticks."

"So what happens if there is trouble on Wednesday, Saturday or Sunday in this town?"

"Oh, they appear when they have to."

"What is your name?"

"Mr. Duncan. Ervin P. Duncan. But most folks call me E. P." The man winked. "I tell 'em it stands for *Exceptional Person.*"

Longarm beat down a strong impulse to gag. "E. P., do you know anything about the theft of United States savings bonds?"

"I'm happy to report that they were recovered," the telegraph operator announced. "The leather pouch of government bonds was found out on the South Road about three miles from Elko, tossed in the brush. But all the stolen cash is still missing."

"How much cash?"

"About eight thousand dollars," E. P. said. "Marshal Nestor says that the Indians took it all to buy whiskey, guns and new horses."

"And what about the murders?"

The man shrugged his narrow shoulders. "There have been four murders in the last six months that I know of. Two of the victims were just Indians and the other two were cowboys. Marshal Nestor thinks that all of them were done by Indians."

"Indians killing Indians?" Longarm asked with skepticism.

"Sure, the Shoshone and Paiutes have been raiding and scalping each other long before the white man came into this part of the country."

Longarm thought to ask the telegraph operator how he knew that for certain but decided not to waste his time. Instead, he said, "It sounds like Marshal Nestor and Deputy Coon have everything all figured out. To their way of thinking, all the troubles are due to the Indians."

"I expect that is about right," E. P. said. "Both the Paiutes and the Shoshone are all up in arms over the horse killings."

"*What* horse killings?"

"Why the mustangers! A whole bunch of them arrived in this town last summer and they've been trapping wild mustangs by the score in and around the Ruby Mountains. The Indians aren't real happy about that because they claim the mustangs belong to them. They are mad as hell."

"I see."

E. P. leaned forward and lowered his voice, even thought they were they only ones in the telegraph office. "Everyone here . . . including yours truly, Mr. Excellent Person, is very, very nervous. The Paiutes and Shoshone never have gotten along. They fight all the time. But now it sounds like maybe they're getting together to start warring on us whites. If they do, a lot of blood is going to be spilled in this country, starting with that of Mr. Drummer's mustangs."

"Who is Mr. Drummer?"

"Why, Spike Drummer is the most powerful rancher in

Elko County. He runs more cattle than you could shake a stick at. And he *hates* wild mustangs. Says they ruin his water tanks and eat his grass. So Mr. Drummer hired this bunch of mustangers to clean them out."

Longarm's head was beginning to ache. The more he listened, the more he disliked this whole miserable Nevada assignment. Damn Billy Vail! Couldn't the man just once assign him a simple case?

Longarm started for the door, but the telegraph operator's voice caused him to pause when he said, "Five Indians were killed last night right here in town. Their bodies were discovered behind the livery. From what I hear, they were all hanged to death. They haven't even been cut down from their nooses. There is a big crowd over there waiting and watching, but they're trying to keep the children away. Everyone is so morbid!"

Longarm felt a sudden tightening in his gut and a flush of fury. "Any idea who hanged the Indians, or why?"

"No," the telegraph operator replied. "Everyone is waiting for the marshal and his deputy to return from rabbit hunting and cut those Indians down. Most of the town is saying, 'good riddance.' But the smart people like me are worried sick that, when they learn of what happened, the Paiutes and the Shoshone are going to come on a raiding party and burn half of Elko to the ground."

"Are there enough of them to do that?" Longarm asked.

"You bet there are," the man said, with a grave expression. "Didn't you notice all the woman and children that boarded the train for Reno when you got off it just a few minutes ago?"

"I didn't," Longarm admitted.

E. P. said, "I'd board it myself, but I got this job to do. Even so, I put my missus on the train just before you arrived. Her and our children. And now I'm keeping a shotgun close at hand."

The man lifted a battered double-barreled shotgun and

stupidly pointed it at Longarm who yelled, "You idiot, turn it away from me!"

E. P. slammed the gun down on the counter. "Take it easy, Marshal Long, the gun isn't even loaded yet."

Longarm growled, "If you counted all the dead men shot by what they thought were empty guns and rifles, you'd fill a ten-acre cemetery. My advice is to get rid of that thing before you accidentally kill yourself or someone like me."

"I'll keep it, if you don't mind."

"Send the telegrams," Longarm said, angry and edgy with too much on his mind. "And don't forget what I told you about secrecy."

E. P. said something, but Longarm didn't hear it as he headed for the Elko Hotel. He would quickly check in and then he was going to the livery, where he'd cut those five hanged Indians down.

What the hell kind of a place *was* Elko?

Chapter 11

Elko was a fine little railroad and ranching community spawned in 1869 when the Central Pacific Railroad was racing eastward in a desperate race with the Union Pacific. And, like most hastily built railroad towns created by the great transcontinental railroad race, Elko had been thrown up in a haphazard manner, with many of the original buildings little more than wooden storefronts behind which stood dirty canvas tents. But while so many other railroad towns had boomed and quickly gone bust, Elko had endured and even prospered, thanks to a railroad repair station and the excellent grazing land which had given rise to a thriving cattle industry.

Now, however, as Longarm left the hotel and marched down the street toward the gawking crowd, he was thinking no kind thoughts about Elko. It seemed the town had grown malignant and the source of its deepest cancer was yet to be determined. Or perhaps there were many cancers, one of them being a hatred of the red man and another greed by a ranch owner named Spike Drummer.

Longarm could see the fringes of the morbid crowd as he approached, but it wasn't until he rounded the corner of the livery that he got the full effect. *My god,* Longarm thought, *there must be three hundred damned people here staring at the five dead Indians!*

The Indians were not only dead, but their faces were bloated with dark blood, giving them a hideous appearance. Some of them had evacuated their bowels and the stench of urine, feces and death clung heavily in the still, corrupted air.

Longarm felt anger giving way to rage. He drew his Colt revolver, raised it in the air and fired twice. The crowd, already tense, jumped as a single body and whirled around.

"I guess I got your attention!" Longarm shouted. "Why in the hell are all you sick townspeople staring at those poor, dead Indians! Someone cut them down!"

A beefy-looking man wearing a good suit emerged from the crowd to confront Longarm. "And who are you to yell and berate the good citizens of Elko?"

Longarm tore his badge from his coat pocket and raised it up so that everyone in the crowd could see it. "I'm United States Deputy Marshal Custis Long and I want you to cut those bodies down immediately!"

"Can't do that. Got to wait for our own marshal to inspect 'em first," the man said, sticking out his chin with belligerence.

Longarm shoved the man hard and he reeled into the crowd. "You," he grated, "cut them down."

"The hell with that!"

Longarm reached into his pants pocket and pulled out his barlow knife. He opened a razor-sharp blade. "Do it now or I'm going to kick your butt up between your shoulder blades and then I'm going to arrest you."

"What for?"

"For . . . for being an insensitive shit!"

The man blustered. "I'm no insensitive shit! I'm Mayor John Coleman!"

Longarm raised the knife and pointed it at the mayor's face. "Are you going to do it or am I going to have to . . ."

"OK. OK!"

The crowd parted as Coleman tore the knife from Longarm, cutting himself in the process. "Ouch! I need a doctor!"

"Cut 'em down first," Longarm hissed. "Or that cut hand will be the least of your many injuries."

"You're making a big, big mistake."

"Not as big as you've already made," Longarm shot back at the man.

The mayor flushed with anger and yelled for some men to pull an unhitched buckboard over so that he could climb onto it and get to the bodies.

The first Indian landed on his face and bounced, giving off a putrid gas. Several women in the crowd fainted. Several men vomited. Others turned and started to rush away.

"Everyone stay right where they are!" Longarm shouted. "You came to see death, then by god you're going to see it all the way."

A pretty young woman moaned and collapsed. A fat woman pulled her two children to her and cursed Longarm. He didn't care. Longarm was so furious that he wanted to shoot the whole bunch of them.

"Cut the rest down, Mayor Coleman!"

The mayor had turned green. Up close to the corpses, the stench was horrific and the bodies were shrouded with hungry black flies. The mayor cut the next body down and then he tossed his stomach and fell to his knees heaving. Longarm's jackknife fell from Coleman's hand and was retrieved.

"You. You and you!" Longarm shouted, pointing at three other men.

Longarm could see that they wanted to run but dared not because of his trembling, terrible rage. So they jumped up on the buckboard and cut the other three bodies down.

Two more women fainted. Children were wailing, horrified by the spectacle. Longarm suddenly felt his rage disappear, to be replaced by sadness and a touch of guilt. "All right. Everyone get the hell out of here, right now!"

The mayor climbed unsteadily to his feet and his face was ashen. "Marshal, where are you from? I'm going to make sure that you lose your badge. I'll also make damn sure that you are arrested for assault! We have a local constable and deputy and by damned they will arrest you or lose their jobs!"

"Mayor Coleman, you thoroughly disgust me. So don't give me a reason to beat you to a bloody nubbin," Longarm hissed.

The mayor suddenly realized he had vomit all down the front of his suit coat. He tore it off and hurled it into the dirt, then changed his mind and picked it up again. "You'll be sorry for this," he whispered, in a voice that shook.

Longarm raised his pocketknife and the man recoiled, then turned and hurried after the crowd. After a few minutes, he was alone . . . or so he thought.

The Indians had been hiding behind another building. Now, seeing Longarm standing by himself, they appeared. Ten, maybe a dozen. Their faces were twisted with hatred as they came forward. Longarm drew his Colt but let it dangle at his side.

The Indians came to a halt before him and their leader, a man with black-and-silver hair, said, "You lawman get off train?"

"That's right. I'm from Colorado and I've been sent here to stop what looks to me like the start of a war that your people cannot win."

"We kill white men who do this," the leader said, his bloodshot eyes never leaving Longarm's face. "My name is Chief Niawah."

Longarm turned and studied the others. He did not know if they were Paiutes or Shoshone, and it really didn't matter at the moment. One mistake and Longarm had no doubt that he would be a dead man.

"Listen, Chief, I'm going to find out who did this and see that they hang for murder."

"Ha!"

Just that. Just a short bark that said more than a thousand words and told Longarm that Niawah did not believe him.

"I give you my word that I will find out who murdered those five men and see that they are hanged."

"Liar."

The word was flat, contemptuous and uncompromising. Longarm knew that what he said next would count for everything.

"Chief, I need time to find out and arrest those responsible for this . . . this awful crime."

"You are a white man. No justice. All lies."

"No," Longarm argued without heat. "I'm not a liar. I'll find out who did this and bring them to justice. Hangman's justice. That is my promise."

The Indian's black eyes seemed to penetrate Longarm's skull, seemed to reach into his mind and his heart. Finally, the Indian chief gave a small nod of his head. "I give you until the rise of the full moon."

One of his men objected. But the objection was quickly silenced by a movement of the older man's hand.

"But Chief Niawah," Longarm protested, "that's just seven or eight days. Hardly more than a week."

"I *know* who killed my people."

Longarm looked the Indian right in the eye. "Tell me."

The chief turned and spoke to his companions and gave orders. Instantly, his men wrapped the hanged Indians in blankets and tied them to their ponies.

"Tell me who is killing your people," Longarm urged. "I need to know where to start."

"I am Paiute," Niawah said proudly. "We have many horses. Many mountains and much good water."

"I am glad," Longarm said. "And what of the Shoshone?"

The question seemed unexpected and Niawah was slow

to answer. "Sometimes enemy. Sometimes friend."

"What about here and now?"

"Friend," Niawah grunted. "Shoshone and Paiute against white men who come on our lands and take our horses."

"Wild mustangs," Longarm told the man. "They belong to whoever catches them."

"*Indian* ponies! White man catch in pens and then treat ponies very bad. Send them to train. Send them to big place where they are slaughtered just for *dog* food!"

Longarm knew this to be largely fact. Some mustangs were broken and made into good, sturdy little mounts for both civilians and the cavalry. They were renowned for their sure-footedness and their toughness. They could carry a man day after day through the roughest, rockiest country where Eastern-bred horses would turn up lame. They could live and even thrive off the desert shrubs, weeds and poor grasses that would soon turn an Eastern horse into a skeleton. But, despite all those sterling qualities, most mustangs ended up as feed for dogs, hogs and chickens.

"This is true, Chief Niawah," Longarm said. "And it is a shame. But . . ."

"Listen, not talk!" the chief interrupted. "I tell you something one time only."

"Sorry," Longarm said. "I'll listen well."

"Come," the old man ordered, motioning Longarm off toward a corridor between the livery and another building, where they could have privacy.

Longarm reluctantly followed the Paiute, wondering if Chief Niawah had a few more of his white-hating warriors hiding there, ready to slit his throat and take his scalp.

Chapter 12

Chief Niawah studied Longarm closely as they stood between the buildings and out of sight from the townspeople. The old Paiute said, "Many white men hired by Drummer have come onto our lands to catch and take away our mustangs. My people killed some of them but more come. They catch five of my warriors in Echo Canyon up in what you call the Ruby Mountains. Bring them here last night and hang them."

"Do you know exactly which white men did this thing?" Longarm asked.

"No. We track horses here. Find warriors all dead. Now, we go to war with mustangers hired by Drummer." The old chief's face turned to stone. "We hang them! Torture them first."

Longarm shook his head. "That would be a big mistake. The soldiers would come and there would be a war that you cannot win."

"Shoshone will help Paiute. We know how to fight and how to hide. Pony soldiers no catch and kill Indian. We kill *all* pony soldiers."

"Chief Niawah," Longarm said, choosing his words

with great care, "you must not kill the men who hanged your warriors. I will make sure that they pay for their crimes."

"You promise they hang?"

Longarm had to be honest. "I cannot give you that promise," he admitted. "We have to have proof, and then the fate of the men who did this terrible thing is in the hands of a judge and jury."

"White judge! White jury!"

"Yes," Longarm said quietly.

Niawah spat on the ground between their feet. "We kill mustangers and we kill Drummer. If pony soldiers come, we kill them all."

Longarm could see that he was not going to change the old Paiute's mind, so he stopped trying. "I will come out to your land and catch the ones who hanged your warriors. I will come tomorrow."

"Maybe you die, too."

It was a test of his courage. Longarm saw that the chief was waiting for a reaction, but he wasn't going to get one. Not even the blink of Longarm's eye.

"Where are your people to be found?"

"Everywhere. The mountains and the deserts. The valleys and beside the rivers."

The chief did not seem to be willing to trust Longarm. But he did turn and face the northeast, toward the Ruby Mountains. "I will find you, then."

Chief Niawah nodded and then he was gone. Longarm heard the sound of beating hooves.

Longarm went back to the Elko Hotel. It was a nice, two story structure with chandeliers in the lobby and clean sheets on the beds. "Any messages for me?" he asked the hotel desk clerk, hoping that he'd heard back on his telegrams.

"No, sir."

"I'll want hot water in the tub up there for a bath."

"Yes, sir."

"And I'm expecting a telegram from Denver."

"Yes, sir."

"You'd better not read it."

"No, sir!"

"Good." The desk clerk looked frightened and upset and must have already heard all about the hangings and confrontation that had just taken place behind the livery stable between Longarm and the mayor. No doubt he was wishing that this new federal marshal had chosen one of Elko's other hotels.

Longarm went up to his room, removed his coat and tie and kicked off his boots. He was going to shave and take a hot bath, then a nap. After that, he'd go find out if the local sheriff and his deputy had returned from their rabbit hunting.

"Rabbit hunting," Longarm snorted with disgust. "And last night five men were hanged. Would you believe that?"

Longarm's bath was a welcome diversion. You could take a bath in first class on the Union Pacific railroad, but it cost a small fortune, so he'd passed. Now, however, it was cheap and the water was hot and steamy. When he was finished, Longarm stepped out of the tub and grabbed a waiting towel.

Suddenly, there was a loud and insistent rapping on the bathroom door. "Hey, are you in there?"

"Who are you looking for?" Longarm said, reaching for the gun he was never without.

"I'm Marshal Orvis Nestor! Are you that interfering federal marshal?"

"I'm a federal marshal."

"Open the damned door! I got something to say to you and I want it to be face-to-face!"

"No," Longarm said, not appreciating the man's tone of voice.

"Open it or I'll break it down!"

"You try that, Marshal Nestor, and I'll make sure that you're blowing soap bubbles out your butt for at least the next week."

Orvis Nestor had not been expecting such a bold and threatening response. There was a moment of silence before he growled, "I'm going back to my office. I expect you to be there in less than thirty minutes."

"I'll be there," Longarm told the man. "Say, did you bag any jackrabbits today?"

"Huh?"

"While we almost had a mob scene and a bloodbath in your town, did you and your deputy shoot any jackrabbits?" Longarm asked, not bothering to hide his sarcasm.

"Screw you!" Nestor hissed. "You're already on my shit list, so I wouldn't be acting like a smart aleck, buster."

"Custis Long," Longarm said, correcting the man. "My name isn't 'Buster.' Never has been and never will be, Orvis."

"Wise ass," Nestor spat as he tromped back down the upstairs hallway. Longarm could hear the heavy thud of the local constable's boots all the way down the stairs and into the lobby.

"This kind of ignorant local horseshit," Longarm muttered to himself as he vigorously toweled his muscular frame, "is what makes me think I ought to return to Denver on the first train going back East, then marry Lilly and hand in my badge."

Longarm took his own sweet time in his hotel room. He polished his boots, wiped his coat and trousers of dust and made himself as presentable looking as he possibly could. Just before he left the room and headed downstairs, he fired up a cigar and made sure that his Colt was ready and resting exactly where it would jump into his hand.

"Marshal?" the desk clerk offered in a small voice. "You have two telegrams waiting."

"Good!" He took it from the man, went over to one of the lobby's overstuffed chairs and sat down. The telegrams were in sealed envelopes, and when he opened the first one he found an authorization for another hundred dollars, which was to be taken to the local bank for disbursement.

"Thanks, Billy," Longarm said with more than a small measure of relief.

Billy Vail's message was short and cryptic.

> *You were not sent West to solve any other murders than those that are taking place in Elko. What about the stolen government bonds? Focus on your assignment and inform me daily of your progress.*

"Daily? Ha!" Longarm said. "You'll be lucky to hear from me in the next week."

He opened Lilly's telegram, not sure what news it might contain.

> *Darling Custis.*
>
> *I am so happy that the garnet saved your bacon, especially your delightful hot sausage! I am sending all my love and can't wait to see you again. Be ever so careful.*
>
> *Lilly*

" 'Delightful hot sausage'?"

Then it hit Longarm what she was referring to and he laughed out loud. "Oh, Lilly," he said softly to himself, "with any encouragement at all you could develop a very ribald sense of humor."

Longarm folded both telegrams and placed them in his coat pocket. He checked his gold watch and saw that it was too late to go to the bank for the hundred dollars, which was probably just as well. He didn't want to push the local law over the brink and have them do something rash.

"Nestor's office is just down the street to the right," he said across the lobby, "isn't it?"

"Yes, sir!" the anxious desk clerk called. "Two blocks down. You can't miss it."

"Did the people of Elko really elect that clown to office?"

The desk clerk shrugged. "Marshal Nestor has always discouraged competition for his office. Same goes for Mayor Coleman."

Longarm shook his head in puzzlement. "You people sure drew a couple of duds in those two. The mayor and your marshal strike me as idiots. Why don't you run yourself?"

"For marshal?" The desk clerk nervously giggled. "I can't even shoot straight."

"Then why not run for mayor?"

"Because I'm not a politician and I hate public speaking. Besides, I'd never win. Mayor Coleman has the support of the most important business and ranching people."

"Well," Longarm said, "someone ought to step forward and replace those two. Maybe I'll encourage Nestor and Coleman to resign."

The man's eyes widened with surprise, then confusion. "They would *never* resign."

"Oh," Longarm said as he headed toward the door, "you never can say that. Good things happen that you never expect. And, in addition to all the other problems you have with the Indians and murders, Elko sure needs a thorough housecleaning."

Longarm started down the busy main street, aware that he was being stared at by everyone in sight. Two rough-looking cowboys stepped into his path on the boardwalk. Longarm thought they were going to try and block his path, perhaps make him step off the sidewalk into the street.

He reached across his belly and placed his right hand on the Colt he wore on his left hip, butt forward, did it casually and with a smile on his face. "Afternoon, gents," he said, his hand tightening a little on the Colt. "You boys have something you want to say to me?"

If they did have some smart remark it quickly left their

100

minds. And when Longarm stepped in closer, they parted like the Red Sea. He didn't turn around to protect himself because he knew that they were not real killers, only a couple of mustangers that had gotten liquored up for courage.

Longarm continued down the boardwalk. It was a nice, sunny day, although the wind was blowing dust around on the street. That wasn't the least bit important. There were going to be a lot of things going on before the damn dust finally settled in Elko, Nevada.

Chapter 13

Longarm didn't bother to knock on Nestor's door. He just grabbed the handle, twisted it hard and shoved it open with a bang. The marshal and a man that Longarm took to be his deputy jumped out of their battered office chairs. Nestor had been drinking a cup of coffee and it spilled on his shirt. Deputy Coon had been smoking and, in his haste to get himself upright, he knocked his cigarette flying.

"Sonofabitch!" Orvis Nestor bellowed. "Ain't you ever been taught to knock before you enter? Bargin' in here like that could get a man shot!"

"Or scalded," Longarm said, eyes on the spreading coffee stain.

Nestor was the shortest of the pair, but he was fit and pugnacious-looking with a crooked nose, some notable facial scars and round, muscular shoulders. He looked like a thug and a brawler. A dangerous man in a fight. His deputy, Don Coon, reminded Longarm of a mournful coonhound. He was tall, loose-skinned and angular, with immense bags under both of his sad but wary eyes. Both men appeared to be in their mid-thirties and neither of them was interested in cleanliness.

The office stank of things that Longarm did not want to

even think about. It was also disorganized, like the men themselves.

"I'm United States Deputy Marshal Custis Long," he said, knowing better than to stick out his hand and offer to shake. "I've been sent here from Denver to see if I can help you officers get things under control."

"We got 'em under control," Nestor snapped. "And we damned sure don't need the likes of you threatening the townspeople."

Longarm forced a tight grin. "Nestor, you must be referring to that situation behind the livery. The one where five Paiute Indians were hanged, but no one had decency to cut them down much less send for an undertaker or the law."

Nestor's deep-set and closely spaced eyes blazed with hatred. "I already don't like you," he said. "And I sure don't appreciate someone coming into my town acting like they were some kind of gawdamn *king!*"

Longarm could see that there was no sense in mincing words or trying to win this man's cooperation. "Look, Nestor, we can do things two ways. First, we can work together and try to get a lid on this mess you have in Elko . . . or, we can work separately. If your pride and stubbornness force us to work separately, I'm going to do everything in my power to make sure . . . when this is all wrapped up . . . that you and your deputy are fired."

"The hell you say."

"The hell I do say," Longarm told them, knowing his statement had jolted them hard.

Longarm continued. "If you help rather than stand in my way, we might just make things easier all the way around and you'll keep your jobs. So which is it to be?"

His little speech had certainly rocked the two lawman back on their heels. Finally, it was the deputy, Don Coon, who exclaimed, "You ain't got the authority to fire us! You're a nobody from Colorado. You're just blowin' smoke."

"Is that what you think? Well, I may be from Colorado, but I *am* a federal officer. And, the last I'd heard, Nevada was still a part of the United States. That means that I have authority here. And you might as well also know that my boss is good-friends with the governor of Colorado, who happens to be best friends with your Nevada governor."

Longarm didn't know if his governor even knew the Nevada governor's name, but it sounded impressive.

The two exchanged quick and worried glances. Finally, Marshal Nestor said, "What do you want?"

"The same thing that I hope you want," Longarm told the man. "Elko is a powder keg. This country is on the verge of a war between the red man and the white. Do you really think the Paiutes and Shoshone are going to let mustangers hang their people without retaliating?"

"We'll wipe them redskins out once and for all," Coon bragged with a confident sneer. "Those damned Digger Indians are nothing but vermin. They have a reservation up at the Ruby Mountains, but they think they own the whole state. Both the Paiutes and Shoshone hunt when and where they please. They cut ranchers' fences, steal and eat their cattle, rustle their horses. The sooner they're all wiped out the better off this country will be."

Longarm had heard a lot of Indian-haters in his time, but Don Coon was as vehement as any. "Are those also your sentiments, Marshal Nestor?"

"You bet!"

"Then I guess this conversation is finished," Longarm told these sorry excuses for lawmen. "I don't want anything to do with either of you birds. And if you get in my way during this investigation of murder and robbery, I'll make sure that neither of you ever wear a badge again."

"The hell you say!" Nestor shouted, taking a menacing step forward as he balled his fists. The Elko marshal wasn't as tall as Longarm, but he was stocky and itching for a good fight.

"Don't," Longarm warned, seeing a glint of anticipation in Nestor's beady eyes. "Don't even think about taking a swing. If you do, I'll make sure that you go to prison."

Marshal Orvis Nestor halted. His face was red and his lips trembled with fury. "Get out of my office!"

"Gladly." Longarm turned to leave, hand resting on the doorknob. "I'm going to find out who murdered those five Paiutes, and when I do I'll need the temporary use of your jail."

"You'll get it when hell freezes over!"

"That's about what I expected to hear," Longarm said, his lips twisted in a show of distain. "And it's fine. It'll make things simpler."

"What do you mean?" Coon demanded, suddenly looking worried.

"Well, I mean it will be simpler if you and the murderers are in that cramped and filthy jail locked up together. Then, I won't have to worry about getting ambushed."

Nestor cursed, but Longarm laughed as he went out the door.

"Hey, Federal Lawman!"

Longarm's hand flew to the gun on his left hip.

"Easy!" the voice said. "I'm friendly."

He turned to see a buxom woman in a green satin dress standing in the doorway of a small saloon. Her hair was red and piled up high on her head. She was probably in her middle twenties, still pretty but with the telltale signs of a hard life of whoring already showing on her heavily rouged face.

"You shouldn't startle a man like that," Longarm said as he relaxed.

"Sorry, but I don't want to be seen talking to you."

"Why?"

"Because, Marshal, you'll be leaving soon . . . either dead or alive."

"I guess that's the truth," Longarm said. "But it'll be alive, thank you, ma'am."

"Listen, Marshal, could you please come around to the back alley? I'd like a few words with you in private."

The woman stayed hidden in the shadows of the doorway.

Longarm didn't want to be lured into some alley and then be ambushed. "What's this about?"

"It's about what is going on in Elko. Are you interested?"

Longarm decided to take the bait. An opportunity like this might not come along again. "Sure," he said, continuing along the boardwalk.

Marshal Nestor and his deputy might be watching him closely . . . in fact they probably were watching him with suspicious, hating eyes. So Longarm walked to the end of the block and then glanced up at the signs, as if he were seeking a particular business establishment. Only when he was sure that he could not be seen from the marshal's office did he turn and hurry up the alley.

The woman in the green satin dress was hiding in her back doorway, barely visible. She was, Longarm realized, very, very cautious. That told him two things. She was frightened of the law in this town, and she was also smart.

"Hey, Big Boy," she said, managing an anxious smile. "Step inside."

Longarm drew his gun. "No offense, ma'am. I've just learned to be careful when I enter someone's back door."

She laughed, but it sounded forced and brittle. "Good thinking, Marshal. But I'm not your enemy. In fact, I may actually be the only friend you have in Elko."

Longarm kept his gun in his fist as he entered the rear of the saloon. It was filled with the usual supplies and beer barrels. He let his eyes adjust to the gloom for a few seconds, then eased his back against the wall so that he could not be sneaked up on.

"All right. What do you want to talk to me about?"

"My name is Bonnie Bucker," she said without pream-

107

ble. "I'm the sole owner of this saloon, and although it may not be the most impressive saloon in this rough-and-gone-to-hell town, it is the most profitable."

"Profit is good," Longarm said, wondering what Bonnie Bucker's real name was before she'd become a woman of ill repute, most likely at a very young age. She was still quite the looker, but he figured that would only last a few more years and then she would age fast from a life of hard drinking and lovemaking.

"Yes, it is," she said, appraising him from his hat to his boots. "But my profits are off lately because of the trouble we're having in Elko. And there are certain people who like a share of my profits and that share is growing because they are greedy and ruthless."

Longarm understood. Bonnie Bucker was being squeezed and he'd bet it was by Orvis Nestor and his dog-faced deputy. It was extortion and the corrupt pair was beginning to take an ever larger share of this woman's saloon profits. Longarm knew it happened often enough, but it always made him disgusted when he learned the extortionists were the very men hired to protect the citizens and business folks. Instead, men like Nestor and Coon bled them dry and then drove them out of town when they could no longer pay the toll.

"You're in a tough situation," Longarm sympathized. "Maybe I can help you out."

A thin and not pleasant smile turned down the corners of her ruby red lips. "And how much would that cost me?"

"Nothing in money. What I need most is solid information," Longarm told her without hesitation. "I need answers and people like you generally know everything that is going on in their town."

" 'People like me' meaning . . . ?"

Longarm quickly backtracked, for he did not want to offend Bonnie. She just might be the key that would unlock all the dirty mysteries he had been sent to solve. "I only meant that men have loose lips when they drink too much in saloons. You own a saloon. You're going to hear a lot of things that most people would never learn. Things that can help me put a lid on this town before it blows sky-high."

She relaxed. "And hard-drinking men also talk too much after they're done screwin'. They want to talk and talk. Once they got their jollies off they usually babble like babes. They'll tell you all the reasons why they're in your bed and not in their own bed with their wives. Tell you how mistreated and mistrusted they are by their ball-bustin' missus. Most of them make me want to puke."

Longarm could see that Bonnie Bucker was not only an attractive, but also a very cynical and jaded woman. That did not bother him. Cynical and jaded was fine. Double-crossing and devious were not.

"What is it they tell you?"

"I don't like standing here in the dark," she said. "My room is upstairs. I don't normally take men up there, but you're going to be an exception. That's also where my best is hidden. Interested?"

"Sure," Longarm said. "Lead the way."

Her upstairs room was secured by a big, expensive lock that took two keys to open and those keys were affixed to a chain around Bonnie's pretty neck.

Longarm followed Bonnie into her upstairs suite, and when she pulled the drapes, he was shocked to see that the place was beautifully decorated. The furniture was all hand-carved, probably by European craftsmen. The chandelier was too large for the room, but it its hundreds of crystals were pink and delicately crafted by a master glass-blower. There was a rolltop desk that would have brought five hundred dollars in Denver, and the rugs were obviously Oriental.

"Nice," he said, noting the French provincial furniture and the original artwork that was almost museum quality.

"It ought to be nice," Bonnie said, going to a liquor cabinet and opening it. "What is your pleasure and don't tell me just plain old whiskey."

"All right. How about a good French cognac? Or some Irish whiskey?"

"Irish whiskey sounds about right," Bonnie said, finding a pair of glasses and then a bottle that Longarm was sure was imported from Ireland. When she had poured the drinks, she raised them and said, "To your good health, Marshal Long."

"And to yours, Bonnie Bucker."

The Irish whiskey was smooth and delicious.

"Have a seat, Marshal."

Longarm eased himself down in an expensive but rather fragile parlor chair. "So what do you want to talk to me about?"

"Marshal Nestor and Deputy Coon."

"Yes," Longarm said, "you said you were being squeezed hard. I expect they are the ones doing it."

"That's right," she told him. "But they are just the underlings. Someone is giving them orders. Telling them how much all the saloon owners can afford. They're smart enough not to kill their golden geese, so to speak. And yet, without profits, why should I or the others bother?"

"Good question."

"The answer is that I and many other saloon owners would sell out and leave this miserable railroad town in a week . . . if we could. But Nestor has made it all too clear that we can't sell. We'd just have to walk away from our businesses. None of us can afford to do that."

"What is preventing you from selling?"

"The minute they find out a place is for sale, it will suddenly catch on fire and burn to the ground. It's happened twice before and no one is so stupid as to think it was accidental or coincidence. Can you imagine this room with this beautiful furniture going up in flames?"

110

He glanced around and shook his head. "No. You must have thousands of dollars invested in this room alone."

"I do," she said, drinking faster than a woman should at that early hour. "But I might as well be living in a prison as here. I'm trapped. I couldn't sell this place for a hundred dollars."

"What can I do for you?"

"Arrest Marshal Nestor and Deputy Coon. Take them away on the train and make sure that they never return."

"It isn't quite that easy," Longarm said. "I'd need solid proof of their extortion. And I'd need it from a good many people who were willing to testify in a court of law."

"I'd do it in a second," Bonnie said, face set and angry. "But the others . . . well, they're afraid of Nestor. Also, they know just the same as I do that the real evil in this town would still be in power. Nestor and his goon deputy would just be replaced. And who is to say if any of our saloons would even be standing when the smoke cleared."

"So we have to bring down the ones in real power."

"That's right."

"And they are?"

"Spike Drummer is the ringleader," she told him. "I'm certain of that."

"And your proof?"

Bonnie tossed the rest of her Irish whiskey down. "I don't have any. I just know that Drummer got that pair into office and he pulls all the strings. He and probably a few corrupt politicians like Mayor Coleman. They've got it all figured out."

"Listen," Longarm told her, "I've got to rent a horse and go out to speak with Chief Niawah and his people. The Shoshone, too, if I can contact them."

"If you're so determined to do that, you'll probably never return to help me."

Longarm managed a smile. "That's a pretty bleak assessment. I spoke with the chief and he seems like a man who realizes he can only lose a war with the whites. But neither will he stand for having his men hanged. He wants . . . and deserves . . . some justice."

"Good luck," Bonnie said. "I think you're too idealistic to expect those Indians to listen to you. My guess is that, if you go to face the Indians, you're a walking dead man."

Longarm had heard enough of that kind of talk. "I'm going now," he said, reaching for his hat. "The best thing that you can do for me is to try and get some proof. Also, speak to the other saloon owners. If you all got together, we could accomplish a great deal. Perhaps even bring down Drummer and the corruption in Elko without firing a shot."

"I'll have to see that to believe it," she told him. "Marshal?"

"Yeah?"

"Do you have any living relatives that you'd like me to notify in case you don't return?"

He thought about that a minute. "There is a young lady in Denver named Miss Lilly Hutton."

"Do you have an address?"

Longarm wrote down Lilly's address as well as his office at the Federal Building with Billy Vail's name. He handed the addresses to Bonnie, saying, "You won't need to contact these people."

"Sure," Bonnie said, "but just in case."

Longarm agreed, thinking that there was no fool like a complete optimist.

Chapter 14

Longarm had a good night's sleep, and early the next morning, a mammoth-sized breakfast. Afterward, he walked back down to a livery different from the one where the hangings had taken place, and inquired about renting a good horse.

"Where you goin'?" the owner, a cheerful little fellow with a long goatee, asked. "And how long will you be needin' the animal?"

"I wish I could say how long, but I can't. I'm hoping no more than a few days, but it could run up to a week."

"You're the new federal marshal, ain't you?"

"That's right."

"Will this be a cash up front deal? Or are you expectin' me to wait for some government pay?"

"I'll give you a voucher."

"I don't want a voucher. Only thing I take is cash, mister."

"But the government *will* pay you."

"What happens if you get killed? Then, I lose my horse, saddle, bridle, blanket and anything else I rent to you. Also, the feds might be upset about you gettin' killed; they could even refuse to honor the voucher."

"But . . ."

"No, sir!" the livery man insisted. "I just can't do it. In

fact, I might not even rent you a horse, if you're goin' someplace dangerous. Which brings us back to my first question—where *are* you going?"

"To find Chief Niawah. I suspect he is in the Ruby Mountains."

The little man shook his head. "You're headin' for your burial, Marshal. That old Paiute is going to take your scalp."

Longarm had heard enough. "I'll rent a horse and saddle someplace else," he told the livery owner. "I've got no time to argue or listen to your dire predictions."

"There's only one other livery in town and old Gabriel won't rent you a horse. He's the most cautious man ever lived and the crookedest. He'll try to sell you a wind-broke horse for three times its true value."

Longarm had not expected this kind of resistance. "If you won't rent me a horse and saddle, what's the cheapest animal and saddle you have for sell?"

"Now we're talkin'," the man said, sticking out his hand. "Name is Casey McDuff. And I do happen to have a couple of cheap horses and saddles. Might be just what you are lookin' for."

"I'll bet," Longarm said, not liking the way this conversation had turned. "Look, Casey, I'm waiting for some money to be wired from Denver. It should be here today, but it might come tomorrow."

"I'll hold your horse for as long as you want," the Irishman said, sounding magnanimous. "But no cash, no horse. You understand that from a businessman's point of view, don't you, Marshal?"

"Sure," Longarm said peevishly. "Let's take a look at your cheap horses."

"Good enough! But you can't be expectin' too much. What we have cheap here are mustang ponies broke by the Indians and sold to me when their owners get tossed in the caboose and can't go bail. Now, some of these ponies may look a bit rough, but they're tough little buggers. Take you

114

to the Ruby Mountains and back and not so much as break a sweat."

Casey was saying all this as they went around his main barn to a pole corral, where they stopped. Casey hung his boot heel on the lowest rail and said, "There they are, Marshal. Fifty dollars and you can take your pick."

There were six or seven mustangs in the pen and they were the sorriest lot of horseflesh that Longarm had ever witnessed. All of them were thin as a bed slat and mangy as reservation mutts. One had a bad eye, another a crooked foreleg. A third was so wild it tried to crash through the corral poles and escape.

Longarm shook his head in disgust, "Fifty dollars! I wouldn't give you half that for the whole lot."

"Well," Casey said, "maybe I could sell one for a mite less than fifty."

"The only mustang I see that looks like it could carry me to the end of the street is that pinto."

"You got an excellent eye for horseflesh, Marshal. Excellent eye! Yes, sir, that pinto is the cream of the crop."

"He's the dregs of the barrel is more like it," Longarm said, focusing his attention on the pinto. "But he is the best-looking horse of the bunch. Is he broke to ride?"

"Ha! He's as broke as you appear to be at the moment!"

"How about I give you my hat and coat as insurance that I'll pay when I return."

"Ha! I'd look like a dummy wearing something so big. No, sir. I regret to say, it's cash on the barrel. But I'll let you have the pinto, a saddle, bit, bridle and blanket for fifty dollars."

"Throw in a sack of grain, halter and lead rope and you've got a deal. Oh, and I want that pinto shod."

"My Lord, Marshal, nobody shoes mustangs! They're born with feet harder than diamonds."

Longarm folded his arms across his chest so that this man would understand that he was not going to compro-

115

mise. The mustang might indeed have feet harder than diamonds but putting shoes on him would just be extra protection. There was nothing worse than having your horse go lame in hard country a long way from civilization.

"I insist that the pinto be shod and I'll check to make sure that the job is done properly."

The liveryman snapped. "Gonna cost you another five dollars. Take the deal or leave it, I don't care."

Longarm was a good judge of men and he could tell whether they were bluffing or not. This little Irishman wasn't bluffing.

"I'll take it," Longarm said. "Let's see the saddle and the rest of the tack I'm buying for such an outrageous sum of money."

The saddle was a disaster. The horn had been broken, probably when a bronc flipped over backward. The leather was so rotten and it had been tacked onto the rawhide tree so frequently that even the tack heads were worn shiny. One of the stirrups was ready to fall off and the tie strings had been chewed away by rats. "I wouldn't ride that thing from where we are standing to your barn."

"Dammit, Marshal, you are a fussy man!"

"Not fussy," Longarm corrected. "I just like things that I pay cash for to work. When they break, as this saddle sure will in a few miles, I get testy. I start feeling that I've been cheated and then I want to get even. You don't want me to come back and get even, do you, Casey?"

"I doubt you will come back at all, Marshal. But . . . all right. I'll show you a much better saddle. Cost you only five extra dollars. Make it an even sixty and you'll ride out of Elko in grand style. Indians will respect you more if you don't come upon them looking like a long-lost beggar."

"Let's see the saddle."

When Longarm went back to the telegraph office, there was a message from Miss Hutton that read:

116

My darling, Custis.

I am so sorry that you had to kill a man on the train. I am so worried about you that I am wiring you money for an immediate first-class train ticket back to Denver. Daddy has a good job waiting where you won't have to kill anyone ever again. We can be married this autumn.

All my love. Lilly

Longarm grinned. That Lilly was more than a bit of all right! But since Billy's government money hadn't come yet, he'd have to use Lilly's money to pay Casey for the pinto and tack. Also, he would be needing a rifle, ammunition and supplies. It wouldn't be cheap, but he'd soon be getting federal money and then he'd have Lilly's generous donation to take him home.

Perfect!

"Good news?" the telegraph operator asked.

"Very. I'm leaving for the Ruby Mountains. Hold all messages in strict confidence until my return."

"Don't you want to wire the lady back to tell her you received her funds and marriage proposal?"

Longarm blushed. "Let's just keep things brewing on the stove. Besides, everyone thinks that I'll get scalped out there and never return."

"I've bet five dollars on that," the man said. "The odds are so attractive that I stand to win twenty-five, if you should somehow return."

"Five to one against me, huh?"

"Yes, sir."

"Before I leave, I'd like to put ten dollars on myself," Longarm decided. "Nothing illegal about that."

"No, sir."

"Good," Longarm told the man as he folded Lilly's telegram and went out the door whistling.

117

He wasn't whistling an hour later when he returned to Casey McDuff's livery and saw four men trying to hold down the pinto mustang while a blacksmith tacked on a pair of shoes.

"Holy Hanna!" Longarm exploded. "That horse is an outlaw!"

"Naw," the Irishman said, plucking the sixty dollars from Longarm's hand. "He's just never been shod before. Once he's up and settles down a mite, he'll be fine to ride."

Longarm climbed through the corral poles and hurried over to the scene of battle. Two of the men sitting on the pony looked beat-up and were bleeding. The other pair was clearly frightened.

"This is *your* pony?" one gasped.

"I'm afraid so."

"Good luck," the blacksmith said as he nailed down the last shoe. "He's a biter and a kicker and I'll bet he's also a hellacious bucker."

"Casey!" Longarm shouted, whirling around. "You're going to get on this horse and ride him around this corral or I'm taking back my money and kicking your skinny butt up between your shoulder blades!"

The Irishman looked down at the sixty bucks in his grubby little paw, squared his shoulders, drew up his sagging pants and said, "Sure I'll ride the pinto, Marshal. Let him up and everyone get out of our way!"

The livery owner surprised everyone when he jumped onto the pinto's back and then clung to the saddle while the pinto bucked a few hard ones. After that, however, the horse settled down and began to trot around and around the corral.

"See, a baby could ride this mustang!" Casey shouted to the amazed onlookers.

Longarm sighed. "It looks like I've got the pinto whether I want him or not."

"Looks like," one of the bloodied cowboys agreed.

Longarm gathered up his supplies, sack of grain and newly purchased rifle. He entered the corral and had Casey lengthen the stirrups while he tied on the rifle and gear. "He'd better not pitch me, Casey."

"Just keep his head above his knees," the liveryman advised. "A horse that can't get its head down can't buck much."

Longarm jammed a boot into the saddle and swung aboard. The pinto shivered and shook, and then it stepped out lively. He rode the animal around and around the corral a few times and then shouted, "Open the gate!"

When the gate was opened, Longarm plow reined the pinto toward the opening and the horse laid back its ears and shot forward so suddenly that Longarm nearly went over the back of his saddle. But he got a good, solid grip on the horn and hung on for all he was worth as the horse raced into the street.

"That way!" Longarm shouted as he strained to get the pinto mustang heading northeast toward the distant Ruby Mountains.

He raced out of town as if Satan were nipping at his heels. The pinto nearly ran down an old couple, who did a surprising job of leaping onto the boardwalk to save their lives.

After that, it was all smooth sailing. Longarm let the wild little pinto pony run like the wind, and the animal went at least five miles before he showed the slightest inclination to slow his pace.

"Well, you are sure fast," Longarm said when he finally got the horse to walk, "and it's obvious that you aren't the least bit lazy. I'm going to call you Pronto. And, if we get into big trouble, I'll expect you to live up to your new and well-deserved name."

Chapter 15

Longarm followed the muddy and meandering Humboldt River for about twenty miles, then he cut southeast toward the distant Ruby Mountains, certain that he would find the Paiutes. The pinto mustang he'd named Pronto seemed to be a good riding horse, sure-footed, eager to travel and inexhaustible.

Longarm had once chased a pair of outlaws through this hard, rocky country. Chased them right into the Rubys, which were wild and beautiful. But that had been at least eight years ago, and he was not exactly sure where he was going. The way Longarm saw it, the Paiutes would find him before he'd find them.

Around sunset, he found a spring and some cottonwoods with enough grass to fill Pronto's belly. After some initial difficulty, he hobbled the pinto and gave it enough grain so that the animal would remember him and not move about during the night.

Longarm built a fire and fried some bacon and potatoes for his supper. When the stars came out, he spread his bedroll and listened to the coyotes howl until he grew sleepy. Pronto was eating grass near the spring, and the mustang seemed content enough. Around nine o'clock,

Longarm fell asleep, and he didn't wake up until well after sunrise.

"It looks like a fine day to travel," he told the mustang as he saddled and bridled him. "So let's just forget the bucking stuff and make things easy on the both of us."

Longarm knew that he wasn't a bronc-buster, and that getting pitched way out here in the middle of northern Nevada could pose serious problems. For one thing, if he landed either in sharp brush or rocks, he could be seriously injured. Also, if Pronto managed to run away, he'd be afoot with one hell of a long walk back to Elko.

"So I'll leave the hobbles on while I mount up the first time, just to test the water, so to speak," he told the mustang. "If you behave, then I'll dismount, remove the hobbles and we'll do it all over again."

It seemed the prudent thing to do, so Longarm drew his cinch tight, then made sure that everything was ready. "Easy now," he crooned, putting his left boot in the stirrup a moment before he swung up into the saddle. "That's a fine Pronto! Good boy!"

The mustang twisted its head around and glared at him with its left eye. He didn't look upset, but he didn't exactly look pleased to have a big man on his back again. And when the mustang sort of bunched up as if to buck, Longarm gave it a sharp crack with the ends of the reins across the rump and made sure that he didn't allow the pinto to get its head down. Because he was sure the mustang would and could buck, if given half a chance. The smart thing to do was not to give it a chance.

"There," Longarm said, dragging Pronto's head up. "Why don't we just stand here and settle down for a few minutes. Then, I'll get down nice and easy, get my rifle and gear tied down right and . . ."

Suddenly, Pronto jerked the reins out of Longarm's hands, dropped his head between his legs and started bucking for all he was worth. Longarm lost his right stirrup first, then his left and then he went sailing over the mustang's head, doing a complete, but not graceful somersault.

He landed on flat ground with just a few pieces of rock, none of them larger than his fist. But they were big enough to hurt like hell, and he lit on one of them right behind his ear.

Longarm saw stars, even though it was full daylight, and passed out.

When he awoke, he groaned. He sat up with his head still spinning and he felt as if he'd been run over by a stagecoach.

"Damn that horse!" he wailed, eyes jumping here and there until he saw the little pinto ravaging his sack of oats.

"Hey!" Longarm shouted, "get away from that or you'll founder your damn self!"

Pronto gave him scant attention as he munched the oats.

"Dammit, you nearly broke me in half!" Longarm shouted, somehow managing to climb to his feet. His ears were ringing, and when he put his hand to his head, he felt blood. That told him two things—that he might have a concussion, but that he hadn't been knocked out for very long.

Longarm took a few steps forward and the world started spinning so fast he fell on his face.

Concussion. No doubt about that. He'd been clubbed a time or two and he knew that the damage was serious. It would pass, but it would take a while. Time that he didn't really have anymore.

Pronto had scattered the oats everywhere, which was probably the thing that kept him from foundering. Longarm managed to crawl over to the ripped and now empty grain sack. He scooped up what oats he could, then he crawled over to the spring and dropped his head in the cool, sweet water. Meanwhile, the mustang started grazing. Had it not been hobbled, Longarm was sure it would already be on the run straight for the Rubys.

"I sincerely curse the day I bought you," Longarm

growled at the grazing horse. "I should have known better, after the way you tried so hard to buck off McDuff."

Pronto's ears twitched to drive off a fly and he went right on grazing.

Longarm woke up for the second time that day, and he guessed it was late in the afternoon. Panicky, he looked around to see if he was alone or not, but Pronto was standing with his head low and his front legs hobbled.

"I didn't expect you'd still be here," Longarm told the little horse. "I figured you'd manage to either chew off the hobbles or hop yourself miles and miles away by now."

Pronto's eyes were heavily lidded. He looked to be a little bloated in the belly and Longarm wondered if the thirty or forty pounds of oats had done him in for keeps.

"Stomachache givin' you some pain?" Longarm asked, feeling damned mean about the situation the pinto had placed him in. "Well, if you bloat up and die, then it's exactly what you deserve for bucking me off this morning."

In reply, Pronto passed a long cloud of foul-smelling gas. He followed that with a loud groan.

"Yep, you're in trouble, just like me," Longarm said with no small amount of satisfaction. "So we'll see if either of us survives this mess."

Longarm drank some water and crawled under the shade of a pinion pine. He wasn't hungry and he still felt dizzy and sick to his stomach. He also felt ashamed of himself for getting into such a desperate fix. Hell, he'd come out here expecting to swap hot lead with some murdering mustangers, and all he'd managed to accomplish was to get himself knocked silly.

"Pronto, if I survive, I will shoot you dead and then get on the first train heading toward Denver. I'll give up my badge to Billy and marry sweet Lilly, if she'll still have me and I ain't completely brain damaged."

Pronto cut more wind and stared at him with pain-filled,

glassy brown eyes. Longarm forced himself to eat a few cold biscuits and then he drifted back to sleep.

Longarm awoke with the dawn breaking over the Ruby Mountains and with his vision clear and his ears no longer ringing as though he'd been hammering on an anvil.

"You still here?" he asked the pinto, who was close by, nosing around at the empty grain sack and looking bright-eyed and eager to travel.

In reply, Pronto flicked his ears a few times and then nickered hopefully.

"Nope," Longarm said, "you ate the whole damn sack of oats and that's the end of it. As far as I am concerned, you can . . . dammit, you got into my sourdough biscuits!"

Longarm's hand went to the gun on his side and he had a moment of real temptation to shoot the thieving horse. Blissfully unaware that his life was being held in a delicate balance, Pronto backed up a few steps and waited to see what else good would come his direction.

"Aw, the hell with it," Longarm grunted, holstering his sidearm. "I can't shoot you."

Longarm climbed to his feet, feeling much better, but certainly not up to his usual. He stretched, went to the spring and washed the blood from his head and the dirt from his face, then went off a ways to relieve himself.

Well, he thought, scratching his privates and looking at all the empty land and sky, *this day can't be any worse than the last.*

No sooner had that positive thought passed through his mind than he saw Pronto throw his head up and stare into the distance, nostrils distended and trembling. The pinto saw something and Longarm was pretty sure it was other horses.

Longarm buttoned his britches and hurried over to get his rifle. He didn't know if what was coming in his direction was friend or foe, but it sure paid to be prepared for the worst, which was what he seemed to be getting lately.

He saw dust on the western horizon and that told him that there were many horses coming in his direction. Longarm guessed that the dust was rising about a mile distant, and that gave him enough time to get himself and his things in order.

"Easy, Pronto," he said as he caught up the animal, which was still very interested in the approaching horses.

Longarm got his bedroll tied behind the cantle of the saddle, and then he tied his sack of supplies to his saddle horn. He even picked up the ruined feed sack and stuffed it into his saddlebag. It took less than three minutes before everything he owned was packed onto the horse.

"Let's get up into those rocks and see what we have coming," he told the pinto as he led it from the spring. "When they get close they'll see our tracks, but at least I'll have the advantage of surprise."

They hurried up into the rocks, and Longarm levered a shell into his rifle. He hoped that the new arrivals would be Chief Niawah and his warriors. Maybe they would trade him a good horse for his miserable, bucking pinto.

Ten minutes later, Longarm saw half dozen white men come galloping over the hill and then angle down to the spring. They were tough-looking gents riding strong, athletic horses. All of the riders were heavily armed, and they carried at least three ropes on their saddles.

"Mustangers," Longarm said to himself. "And maybe Indian-hunters as well."

One of the men, tall and lean with silver hair, dismounted first, then started barking orders for the others to set up a camp beside the spring. Suddenly, the man saw Longarm and Pronto's freshly shod tracks.

The leader dragged out his gun and gave a shout of alarm. His cowboys drew their six-guns, and it didn't take them but a second to focus on the rocks where Longarm was perched.

"All right, come out with your hands in the sky!"

Longarm knew there was little choice but to show his face. He couldn't even mount his own horse to try and make a getaway, although he was sure that the men below would have quickly ridden him down.

It's probably the rancher, Spike Drummer, Longarm thought to himself. *Who else could it be?*

Longarm made a quick decision. He pitched his lawman's badge into the brush, where it was not likely ever to be found. The main thing was that he had to appear to be someone other than a federal marshal.

But who?

The only thing he could think of was that he was a traveler heading across this country who had gotten lost. What else could he pose as? He sure wasn't going to convince anyone that he was a lone mustanger or a cowboy. Not with a pinto pony that was giving him fits and no rope on his saddle.

"All right!" he called, cradling his rifle in his arms and rising into full view of the men below. "I'm coming down."

He grabbed his reins and led Pronto out of the rocks looking downcast and defeated. It was best to look that way so that these men would think he was somewhat harmless.

"I thought you were them damned Indians!" Longarm called as he headed down the little hill toward the rough-looking cowboys. "I sure am glad to see you boys! Yes, sir! I *sure* am glad you aren't the murdering Paiutes."

"My name is Spike Drummer, and I own this spring!" the silver-haired leader snapped. "What the hell are you doing so far from the river?"

"I was told that there was better water here and I thought I'd just try and find it," Longarm lied. "That Humboldt River water has been making me and my pinto horse ill. It was giving us the green apple quickstep."

127

"The what?"

"You know," Longarm said, "the scoots!"

One of the cowboys snickered.

"It's bad river water all right," Drummer said, gun still loosely pointed at Longarm. "But that still doesn't give you the right to trespass on my land and use my spring."

"Sorry," Longarm said, trying his very best to look contrite. "I got turned around and lost in all this hard country. I was waiting for sundown to see which direction is east and which is west."

"Jesus!" one of the mustangers swore with loathing. "What a dumb sonofabitch you are!"

His remark caused the others to laugh. Longarm shrugged his shoulders, still playing the helpless fool. "Yeah, I guess I am pretty pathetic."

"Pathetic ain't a big enough word for what you are, mister! Anybody stupid enough to leave the Humboldt River and travel in this Indian country by himself . . . and with an undersized horse like that . . . ought to be shot for being so dumb."

"Easy, Jake," Spike Drummer cautioned the man who was obviously his ranch foreman or the ramrod of this hard-bitten mustang crew. "This fella has made a bad mistake coming out here, but from the looks of him, he's suffered from his foolishness. No need to rub it in."

"Thanks," Longarm said. "I am feeling pretty stupid."

"What were you fixin' to do next?" Drummer asked.

"Well," Longarm said, looking at the unsmiling faces of the other men, "I was going to have something to eat but my horse ate all my biscuits so . . ."

"Jesus Christ!" Jake chortled. "I do think this is the dumbest man I have ever seen in my entire life!"

Longarm had taken about enough of Hank's insults. And yet he sensed that he had better keep a very short rein on his temper.

"The Humboldt River," Drummer said, raising a hand

128

and pointing to the west, "is about ten miles in that direction. I suggest you get moving."

"Do you mind if I fill my canteen first?" Longarm asked. "And I was wondering if you might want to sell me one of your horses and take this one."

"What!" Jake roared. "Why the hell would we give you a good horse in trade for a mustang when we are already catching all the mustangs we want for free?"

"I guess no reason at all," Longarm said. "Except that I do have some cash and this little pinto and I aren't getting along very well. I didn't mean that I expected one of you men to trade straight across."

"How much cash are you carrying?" Jake asked, eyes narrowing.

"About a hundred dollars."

A big grin spread across the foreman's rugged face. "Then I'll swap you horses and take your hundred!"

Longarm swallowed and looked very worried. "I didn't mean that I would give you that much money in boot for the swap. I was thinking more along the lines of trading for a good broke horse, and giving ten or twenty dollars and my mustang. This pinto might look small, but he's tough as a boot."

"Shit!" Jake swore. "I wouldn't give you two bits for that runty sonofabitch. In fact, I think I'll shoot him and let you walk back to the river. How does that sound?"

The foreman dragged out his pistol and Longarm suddenly realized that he had to do something or Pronto was meat. "Hold on, there!"

"What?" Jake demanded.

Longarm turned to the rancher. "It wouldn't be right for your man to just shoot my pony. He may not be all that impressive, but he's mine and I paid cash for him."

Spike Drummer smiled, but without sympathy. "Jake is my ramrod. And if he wants to shoot your horse, I guess he can. It doesn't matter to me one way or the other."

Longarm was still holding his rifle. Now he understood that he could no longer play the helpless fool unless he was willing to let Jake shoot Pronto. And that just didn't sit well at all. Sure, the mustang had his faults, but he didn't deserve to die.

"Look," Longarm told the foreman, "why don't we just talk this out like reasonable men?"

Jake spat on the ground and seemed to be enjoying himself. "I don't like to talk and I've never been reasonable. And furthermore, I just don't like the looks of you. Either you are the stupidest man in Nevada, or you've been lying to us through your damn teeth."

Longarm turned the rifle on the foreman. "I'm about done with your insults. Drop the handgun."

Jake hadn't expected this. His eyes widened with surprise and then he hissed, "Maybe we *both* ought to drop our weapons and see who is the better man. Are you willing to do that or are you scared down to your toes?"

"I'll fight you, if I have to," Longarm told him. "But you drop that gun first."

"Do it," Drummer ordered. "This man won't kill you. If he does, we'll all gun him down."

Jake didn't like the way this was running, but his pride was on the line so he dropped his Colt in the dirt. "Your turn," he said, balling up his fists.

Longarm pitched the Winchester to the rancher and balled his own fists. He was still feeling some of the residual effects of his concussion and he knew he was not up for a hard fistfight, but there seemed to be little choice. The best and only thing he could do was to end the fight in a hurry.

"Come on," Jake hissed, moving forward with anticipation. "Winner gets your hundred dollars of cash."

"But I already own it," Longarm said.

"Tough luck," Jake swore, charging forward.

Longarm knew a brawler when he saw one and he respected but did not fear them. Jake swung a roundhouse right at where Longarm's head should have been but suddenly wasn't. Longarm drove a wicked uppercut that struck just under the ribs and didn't stop until it had moved Jake's guts up a few inches. The big foreman grunted with pain but recovered instantly.

Jake wheeled around and charged again, this time with outstretched arms, hoping to grab Longarm in a bear hug and crush him. Longarm shot a straight left jab that broke Jake's nose and stopped the man in his tracks. He followed the jab with a right cross to the jaw that knocked the foreman over a bush and sent him sprawling into the dirt.

"Well, well," Jake said, slowly getting to his feet and rubbing the blood from his nose onto his sleeve. He spat onto the palms of his calloused hands. "What do we have here? A real fighter, huh?"

"Come and get your dessert," Longarm taunted.

Jake pulled a wicked knife from his boot top. "Maybe I'll just slit your throat," he said.

Longarm glanced at Spike Drummer, but the man wasn't about to interfere. Rather, there was a wild look of feral anticipation in the rancher's face that was almost more chilling than Jake's gleaming knife blade.

Longarm looked around for a weapon or something to help him fend off the knife attack, but saw nothing. And so, as Jake closed in for a killing thrust, Longarm crouched low, grabbed a handful of dirt and sand, and then hurled it into his attacker's eyes.

Jake was momentarily blinded, but he bulled forward, knife slashing. Longarm grabbed the big foreman's wrist and tried to twist the knife loose, but failed. They grappled and wrestled, then Longarm slammed his hip into Jake and threw the big man to the ground. He jumped on Jake, still intent on disarming the man, but they rolled. Longarm felt the knife blade sear his chest, but then he got the upper hand and bent Jake's wrist around.

It was over in the split second that it took for Longarm to throw all of his weight and strength onto the knife, burying it into Jake's belly.

Jake screamed and his eyes seemed to burst from their sockets as his own blade was ripped through muscle and gut. Longarm jumped off the man and reeled backward, sickened and gasping.

"Spike!" Jake cried. "Spike, help me!"

The rancher came over and knelt beside his foreman. He studied the wound and then pulled the knife out of Jake's belly. He wiped the blade clean and tossed it to Longarm.

"Ain't a thing that I can do for you, Jake," the rancher said. "You're finished."

Jake screamed, but Longarm wasn't sure if it was because of the pain or the certain knowledge that he was already a dead man.

"Spike," the mustanger cried. "For gawd sake, help me!"

In answer, the rancher shot his foreman right between the eyes.

Even the hardened mustangers were shocked by the chilling casualness of Spike Drummer's deadly move. Several had their jaws hanging wide open. Others gulped or looked away.

"He was suffering and there was no way that anybody, even a surgeon, could have saved Jake," Drummer proclaimed. "What I did was to help the man. It's what I'd have done for any suffering animal."

Longarm supposed that was true, but he doubted he had ever seen such a cold-blooded executioner as this powerful rancher named Spike Drummer.

Chapter 16

Drummer and his mustangers couldn't seem to quite believe that Jake had not only failed to kill this seeming idiot who had gotten lost in the wilderness, but that he'd also been whipped and killed.

Finally, the rancher said, "Drag Jake's body up into those rocks and cover it up so that the vultures and coyotes don't get to him right away."

"Aren't we takin' him back to the ranch for burial?" one of the men asked.

"What for?" Drummer replied. "Unless you want to haul his stinking carcass fifty miles through this heat, and then dig him a grave."

The man shook his head.

Longarm reached out for his rifle and it was given to him. Drummer studied him closely and said, "I guess you and that pinto mustang can be on your way."

"I didn't want to kill your foreman," Longarm said. "He just didn't give me any choice."

"I saw that. Are you as good with a rope and a gun as you are with your fists?"

"No," Longarm said. "I'm no cowboy and I can't rope for beans."

"What about your shooting?"

"I'm better than passable."

"I can use a man who is accurate with a rifle and has courage," Drummer said. "I underestimated you. We all did, especially Jake. See that skull resting out there on the hill?"

Longarm followed the rancher's eyes and nodded. "It belonged to a deer, I'd guess."

"Or a burro," the rancher said. "There used to be quite a few of them running wild on this range, but we shot them all out five or six years ago. The only things I want eating this grass are my own horses, the mustangs I'll catch and sell for slaughter, and my cattle . . . in about that order."

"I see."

Drummer pointed to the skull that was about fifty yards distant. "Try to hit it with the rifle."

"Sure," Longarm told the man. He was not a crack shot, not even close. But Longarm could generally hit what he aimed for unless he was drunk or too hurried. Now, he took his time and drilled the skull through its forehead. The bone shattered like pottery.

"Good," Drummer said. "Now give me the rifle and show me what you can do with that Colt on your left hip."

"I'm not a fast-draw artist," Longarm warned, snatching out his Colt plenty quick and leveling it on Drummer's chest. "And I'm not a murderer, either."

"You just murdered my foreman."

"No, I killed him with his own knife, in self-defense. Big difference."

"Maybe," the rancher said. "Let's see you hit something with the pistol. Something like that pinto pony of yours, in the head."

"Nope. I don't shoot horses. Dogs either. How about that rusty old bean can over yonder?"

Spike Drummer turned and nodded. "That will do to convince me."

Longarm had always been more comfortable with his Colt. Now he scarcely seemed to take aim as he raised the gun and fired. The bean can bounced a few feet into the air and Longarm had a strong urge to try and shoot it in midair, but wisely resisted. When the can came to rest, he drilled it again. He let it land and then shot it one more time.

"You'll do," the rancher said, with a smile of approval.

Longarm decided it would not do to look eager. "Whoa up, there, Boss! I'm heading back to the Humboldt River and I'm going on to Reno."

Drummer shook his head. "You killed my best shot. You're going to have to take Jake's place for a while. Besides, we crossed tracks with a Paiute war party between here and the big river. They catch you, they'll scalp and torture you."

"Well," Longarm said, looking confused, "I don't know what you have in mind, but . . ."

"I'll pay you fifty dollars for guarding us while we hunt mustangs. It's dangerous work, but we're never going to be far away."

"Why not use one of your own men?" Longarm asked.

"Because I need every one of them to bring in the wild horses, then keep them from busting loose and getting away. All you have to do is to keep an eye out for the Indians. If you shoot a couple, the rest will run. It's just that simple, pilgrim."

"How long do I have to stay on this job to earn the fifty dollars?"

"We'll be out two weeks."

"I dunno," Longarm hedged.

"Mister," Drummer said, "you don't have any choice. You can hire on and earn fifty dollars, or you can join Jake up in those rocks."

To back up the threat, the mustangers pulled their guns.

"I'd be honored to hire on with you fellas," Longarm said quickly. "Plumb honored."

135

"What do you do besides getting lost?" the rancher asked.

"I gamble some. And I like to charm the ladies," Longarm said with a wink.

"Hmmm, well I don't doubt that one little bit. But out here in the Ruby Mountain range country, you won't be doing any gambling or romancing. And the only members of the opposite sex you might see will be some squaw probably missing her teeth from chewing on pine nuts or insects. We call the Paiutes 'Digger Indians' or 'Bug Eaters.' As far as I'm concerned, they're subhumans. We've hanged a few as an example to the rest and I've told my mustangers to shoot them on sight. I'll expect you to do the same."

Longarm had to bite his tongue. It wasn't that he was an Indian-lover, and he had seen many Indian atrocities. However, he'd seen just as many if not more committed by ignorant and greedy white men like Spike Drummer.

"What's your name?"

Longarm said, "Custis Long."

"I place you as having a Southern accent. Were you a Johnny Reb?"

"I was," Longarm said honestly. "But the War is over and I try not to think about it and what I seen . . . and done."

"Amen," Drummer replied. "I was a Union officer. Fought at Shiloh and was with General Sherman's march through the South. It made me realize that a man either has to fight for what he wants, or he'll be mowed down and plowed under."

"That's right," Longarm said.

"And that goes for Indians as well as Mexicans, Negroes and Whites. A man is a man. Jake Turner was a man. His mistake was in thinking you were not. And that is what cost him his life."

"I didn't want to kill him," Longarm said. "But there was no choice."

"You got that one right," Drummer said. "Jake would have shot you and then shot the pinto . . . unless I stopped him. He was loyal and the toughest sonofabitch I ever saw in a fight . . . until I saw you in action."

Longarm holstered his six-gun. "Jake was mean. I'm not."

"I don't give a damn if you are mean or not," Drummer told him, "just as long as you don't mind shooting Bug Eaters and following orders."

Longarm said nothing.

"All right," Drummer said. "Pull your saddle off that pinto and we'll take it along. You can ride Jake's horse. He's a far better and faster animal."

"I'd like to keep my own."

"Why?"

"Because I paid too damn much money for him from that thief in Elko named Casey McDuff!"

Drummer laughed. "Casey got into your shorts, huh? Well, he is a thief but at least he is small time."

Longarm didn't know what that meant, particularly. But since he wasn't up to getting bucked off Pronto again, he was just as glad to ride Jake's horse. It was a line-back dun, a handsome animal and much bigger and taller than Pronto.

"We'll rest here for two hours," Drummer told his men. "Hobble your horses and let 'em graze and drink."

"Can we start a fire and have some coffee and hot food?" a mustanger asked. "I'm so hungry my backbone is chewin' on my belly."

"Yeah," Drummer said. "We can risk a fire. But keep it low and dry. Minimum smoke. Understand?"

"Yes, sir, Mr. Drummer."

Longarm was glad to hear about the fire, the coffee and hot food. With all of his biscuits having been eaten by Pronto he was in no mood to cook, but he still had his appetite, despite Jake's fresh blood on his hands and shirt.

Longarm unsaddled Pronto, then removed the pinto's bridle. "You were a wild mustang once; now I'm giving you the chance to be one again."

For a moment, the stout little gelding stood unmoving, as if it could not quite believe that it was free of ropes, leather and fences. It turned its eyes to Longarm and studied him for a moment.

"Go on!" Longarm told the mustang. In a voice that could only be heard by the pinto, he added, "Head for the wild and free places where you were born and raised. And I'll make sure this bunch never catches you and takes back your freedom. In fact, I'm hoping to take their freedom away."

He gave the horse a gentle slap on the shoulder that sent it racing away.

"Hey!" one of the mustangers shouted. "What'd you do that for!"

Longarm feigned innocence. "He's a bucker and I didn't think we'd want to bother with him."

"He's worth five dollars at the train station," the mustanger said. "Twenty dollars at the slaughterhouse in St. Louis. You should have asked Mr. Drummer before you set him free."

"I bought and paid for that pinto," Longarm told the man. "I guess that gives me the right to do whatever I want with him . . . including setting him free."

The mustanger stared, totally uncomprehending. Finally he shook his head and started to leave, muttering, "You don't belong among us. You're gonna get your due before this is finished."

"Are you going to give me 'my due'?" Longarm challenged.

The mustanger turned around to see Longarm's hand on his gun. He threw up his hands. "Don't get me wrong, fella. I'm a cowboy, not a killer like you are."

"Just keep that in mind," Longarm warned the man.

He turned back to watch the pinto gallop over a hill, tail and mane flying in the breeze. That gave him a good feeling inside, which he did not fully understand. After all, the horse had tossed and given him a mild concussion. It hadn't been a good saddle horse and probably never would have been. There was too much independence in the animal, too much spirit that would never submit to authority.

"Pronto, dammit, you sorta reminded me of me," Longarm said quietly to himself as a faint smile creased his lips.

"Kill that campfire and everybody mount up!" Spike Drummer shouted. "We're moving out."

Dirt was kicked on the campfire, the coffee pot emptied and the skillet swiped at with a handful of sand. In minutes, the mustangers were swinging into the saddle.

"What do I do with my saddle?" Longarm asked the rancher.

The man looked at the saddle and snorted, "Pitch it on the rocks or just leave it for the Indians to find and take. The damn thing is a piece of sorry shit."

Longarm knew that the saddle wasn't much, but he didn't think it was *that* bad.

Jake's horse was impressive and his saddle was custom-made and of the highest quality. Fortunately, the dead ramrod had been about Longarm's height and so the stirrups needed no adjustment. Fortunate because Spike Drummer wasn't the kind to wait for anyone.

"Let's go!" he shouted.

Longarm's new mount seemed to expect that it should ride in the lead, up with Drummer and his horse. The pace they started off at was truly frightening. Longarm was a decent horseman, but certainly not in the category of these professionals. Drummer didn't look to either side as they raced toward the tall blue-green Ruby Mountains.

Longarm could only imagine how this whole mess would end.

Chapter 17

Longarm wasn't looking forward to mustanging ... at least not the way that he figured this mean job was going to be handled. He could tell that these men were hard-bitten and cruel. So he kept his mouth shut and rode close to the head of this grim mustanging crew, toward the Ruby Mountains, wondering just how he was going to handle himself and what was expected of him by Spike Drummer. Once or twice he looked back to see if Pronto might happen to be following, but the pinto wasn't.

"What's that up ahead?" Longarm asked late that afternoon when he was starting to gall against his saddle. He wasn't accustomed or conditioned to long, hard riding like this rawhide-tough bunch. They had just entered a box canyon that was quite spectacular, with high sides all around and lots of grass and pine trees at the end. The place he was looking at was half hidden in those pines and mostly made of rock.

"One of my two ranch houses," Drummer answered. "The other is bigger and closer to the Union Pacific Railroad and Humboldt River. That's where we ship out cattle and mustangs for the Eastern market. But this is what I call my "outpost." We do most of our mustanging and roundups from this ranch. We'll be stopping there for the night and then leaving early in the morning."

"How early?"

"Before dawn," Drummer said. The rancher gave him a probing look. "That a problem for you?"

"Not at all. It's my favorite time of day," Longarm lied.

"Good."

The ranch house was more impressive than it had first appeared.

Drummer said, "The Paiutes and Shoshone Indians used this canyon for centuries. There are rock paintings all over the canyon's sides, crazy stuff with circles, jagged arrows, snakes and such nonsense. When I first won it from them about ten years ago, there were campfire rings and charred bones everywhere. But the coyotes have carried off all the bones and the Indians know we'll shoot them on sight, so they stay away."

"Have they ever attacked?"

"Oh, hell yes," Drummer told him. "They used to come in bunches, both in the day and in the night. I cleared out whatever trees and rocks there were in our line of fire from the buildings so that we had ourselves a fine Indian shooting gallery. Everywhere we shot an Indian we laid a little pile of rocks and set his head on a pole."

Longarm could see a few skulls resting on pine poles, although most of the skulls were gone, leaving only the dead poles. "How many Indians have you killed?"

"I lost count. Jake shot at least ten by himself. He liked to go out to the mouth of the canyon and hide in wait. He took scalps and gave them to his woman just to hear her scream and curse his name."

"I take it that Jake's woman didn't approve of killing and scalping Indians?"

"No. She's a desert Paiute. Good-looking woman that Jake captured up north after he ambushed her mate. Brought her down here tied head to foot. I've done the same thing with 'em. In fact, I have a squaw right now that is young enough to be my daughter."

"Do they ever try to run away?"

"Sure. But we rope and then whip them."

Longarm bit back his disgust. This man treated Indians like animals, and clearly had obviously prided himself on having a few women as captive slaves. Maybe, Longarm thought, he could set them free, if he ever got the upper hand on Drummer and his outlaws.

They all rode their horses into a big pole corral and unsaddled. Longarm saw Indian women and a few old men come out of the rock house to care for the mustanger's weary horses. Then the slave women returned to the rock house.

"You can eat with me tonight," Drummer said. "When I hire a man to protect my interests, I like to know all about him. We can take care of that over supper and whiskey."

"Sure," Longarm said, realizing he would have to do some more creative history about his past.

"Wash up and come inside when my cook hammers iron."

"Fine," Longarm said, looking around and seeing the mustangers head for the spring, where there were dirty towels hanging off tree branches.

A young Paiute woman was staring at him hard. *Jake's woman.*

"He killed Jake," one of the mustangers said to the Paiute. "You understand me? This big fella killed Jake. I guess maybe I'll take you as *my* squaw now."

The Paiute girl must have understood English well enough to know what had happened to Jake and what was going to happen to her next. She spat in the dirt to show what she thought of Jake or even Longarm. She spun around and started to walk away with her buckskin dress tight around her shapely buttocks.

She did not get far. The mustanger ran up behind her

and grabbed her around the waist. He shoved one of his hands up under her buckskins and she yipped then bit the man's forearm and whirled to strike his leering face.

The mustanger balled up his fist and smashed the Paiute girl alongside of the head so hard that she crumpled unconscious to the dirt.

Longarm had seen enough. He took three strides forward, grabbed the mustanger by the hair and slammed the man down backward. When the mustanger tried to tackle one of his legs, Longarm kicked him right in the face. He cried out in pain and attempted to get up, but Longarm kicked him in the balls so hard he must have sent them up to be introduced to the man's tonsils.

That was the end of that trouble. The mustanger collapsed in a pile of pain and wasn't getting up for at least a couple of agonizing hours.

A mustanger who had been watching drawled, "If you put Frank out of commission so he can't ride tomorrow Mr. Drummer is gonna have you skinned alive. We're already short Jake. We can't stand loosing Frank, too."

Longarm turned to see probably the youngest of the rough lot. "What's your name?"

The mustanger couldn't have been more than eighteen and he was suddenly scared. "Derwin," he stammered. "Derwin Cooper."

"Well, Derwin," Longarm said, "the way that I see things, you ride with some real sonofabitches. Now, I probably just broke a few bones in Frank's ugly face. And when he rides tomorrow, he won't be sitting on his face, will he?"

"Course not."

"So my question to you right now is, do you want some of the same boot medicine?"

Derwin took a couple of hasty steps backward. "Shoot no! I just wanted you to understand that if Frank can't ride tomorrow morning, Mr. Drummer is gonna nail your bloody hide to one of these pine trees."

"Then Frank *better* ride," Longarm said, kneeling down beside the unconscious Paiute girl and picking her up in his arms.

"Hey!" Derwin said, "Where you takin' Nita?"

"Up to the ranch house for doctoring."

Derwin shook his head. "If I were you, I wouldn't."

"You aren't me," Longarm snapped.

He carried Nita up to the ranch house and went inside. Longarm didn't see Drummer, but when he met another Paiute woman in the house he shrugged, trying to indicate that he didn't know where to put the unconscious girl down. The woman understood and led Longarm to a spare bedroom. Even in the poor light, he could see that her eyes burned with hatred.

"Don't look at me that away," Longarm told her. "I didn't hit this girl. A fella named Frank did, but he paid for his mistake. I busted him a whole lot harder than he hit Nita. Can you help her out?"

The Paiute woman was in her twenties, and Longarm had no doubt that she was Spike Drummer's captive concubine. She was scrubbed clean and dressed like a white woman, and her hair was long and shiny from regular brushing.

"Put her down on this bed," the Indian woman instructed.

Longarm did that and said, "You speak good English."

"Yes. I learn from a missionary as a girl."

"Are you Shoshone or Paiute?"

"Shoshone. Jake's woman is Paiute."

"She ain't Jake's no longer." The woman stared at him with a questioning look and Longarm added, "I killed Jake. He was far too mean to live."

"Then Nita is now *your* woman."

"Thanks, but no thanks," Longarm said, seeing how

things worked around this place. "I will admit that she's a pretty one, though."

The Shoshone woman said nothing as she left the room. She returned a few minutes later with a basin of water and a washcloth. After her face had been washed and her brow cooled, the Paiute roused with a groan on her lips.

The two women spoke rapidly, although Longarm had no idea if it was the Shoshone or Paiute lingo. Not that it mattered. Nita now understood what Longarm had done on her behalf and managed a smile. There was more talk, and it became immediately clear that the two young women were having some sort of disagreement.

"What's the trouble?" Longarm asked. "And where is Mr. Drummer?"

"Taking hot bath. Drinking whiskey, too."

"Well, that's fine. So why are you two arguing?"

"Nita says that Mr. Drummer will beat her if he finds her in this room. I say that I will help protect her. If she goes back outside among those white riders, they will fight over her. Maybe all use her for pleasure."

"I'd not allow that to happen," Longarm said in a quiet voice.

The rancher's captive Shoshone woman looked straight through Longarm as if she could read his deepest thoughts. Then she said, "You take Nita as your woman."

"I already got one waiting for me in Colorado," Longarm said. "One I might even decide to marry; although I'm not sure if I'll even live to see Miss Lilly Hutton's sweet face again."

The Shoshone woman didn't care about some woman in a place called Colorado. "You take Nita or men will *all* take her. Very, very bad. Beat, maybe kill after riding Nita."

Longarm was tired, saddle sore and worried. The last

thing he wanted was having to take responsibility for this poor Indian girl. On the other hand, he had no doubt that, with Jake suddenly dead, there would be big trouble for Nita if he were simply to abandon her to that bunch.

Suddenly, Longarm heard a roar from down the hallway. He saw the Shoshone woman stiffen with fear; then she darted out of the room. She appeared a few minutes later and motioned Longarm out of the dim bedroom where Nita lay and into a room cluttered with saddles, bridles and old wooden furniture.

"Hey, Custis, what the hell you been doin' now?"

Drummer was naked and dripping water all over the rough plank flooring. He was drying himself off with a towel. One thing for sure, Drummer was in good shape. There was not an ounce of fat on his body, but there was plenty of muscle to go along with more than a few prominent battle scars. "Well," Drummer demanded, "answer me!"

Longarm decided just to spit it out like it had happened. "I just took possession of Jake's woman out by the bunkhouse. One of your boys, a fella named Frank, wanted Nita, so we had to right away settle that issue. It didn't take long at all, Mr. Drummer."

"Dammit, you'd better not have killed Frank like you did Jake!" Drummer bellowed. "Frank is my best roper."

"He's alive, but not feeling well," Longarm admitted. "However, I'm happy to say that he'll probably be able to ride at dawn."

"He'd better be," Drummer growled. "He just damned well better be."

Before Longarm could think of a reply, Drummer tossed his wet towel aside and marched over to a liquor cabinet. "You a drinkin' man, ain't you, Custis?"

"Sure."

"Glad to hear that. I wouldn't have a teetotaler around

me. Wouldn't even let one in my house." Drummer poured two water glasses full of whiskey. Handing Longarm one, he said, "You can drink this in the bath I just left."

"I'll pass on the bath," Longarm said, not wanting to sit in this man's dirty water.

Drummer sat down naked in one of the wooden rocking chairs and raised his glass to Longarm, who returned the favor. The whiskey was a whole lot better than he expected.

"I don't drink cheap shit," Drummer said. "Cigar?"

"Sure, if it's as good as this whiskey."

Drummer shouted for his Shoshone woman to get them cigars, which turned out to be even better than the rancher's whiskey.

"So," Drummer said, "tell me more about yourself."

"Not much to tell; really. I've been knocking around the West for the last dozen or so years. Went up to the Comstock Lode and tried to make my fortune in Virginia City. And, for awhile, I did."

"How? You don't strike me as a miner."

"I'm not," Longarm said, "I was an 'enforcer' up there. You know, I worked for the saloons and collected overdue gambling debts. Sometimes I was called upon to settle disputes. When I wasn't on someone's payroll, I speculated in local mining stocks. That last part was what broke me."

"You like all kinds and colors of women?" Drummer asked, tossing down the last of his whiskey and pouring himself more.

"Sure do."

"Then Jake's pretty little Paiute is yours. You can have her in one of my bedrooms, so long as you're ready to ride a horse instead of Nita at daybreak."

"I'll be ready to ride a horse."

"See that you are," Drummer said. "Now tell me more about yourself and the Comstock Lode. I been there myself, of course. Lost a lot of money one night in the Bucket of Blood Saloon. Met Dan DeQuill and Mark Twain at the

Territorial Enterprise. Kind of fun fellas that liked to drink good whiskey and smoke good cigars, just the same as you and me. But there were some real cheats and double dealers up in Virginia City. I killed a slick gambling man in the alley behind the Delta Queen. He was dealing from the bottom of the deck, but I never could catch him, so I waited for him in the dark and stuck a knife in his sorry gizzard. He danced on his toes and would have howled like a dyin' dog except I slit his throat and then emptied his pockets. Got my money and his, too!"

Spike Drummer laughed as though it had been one of the funniest episodes in his entire life. But Longarm was not in the least bit amused.

"Splendid," Longarm said dryly. "A man after my own heart."

"Yeah," Drummer said, "if someone does you, you do 'em back ten times as hard."

When they finished drinking and were well nigh drunk, Drummer ordered his cook, an older Indian woman, to set the table. Longarm was famished and the stewed rabbit, potatoes and cooked cabbage tasted fine. He ate until his stomach felt ready to burst and then he watched Drummer, still naked as a jaybird, take his woman and stagger down the hallway.

"Be up and ready at daybreak," the rancher shouted.

Longarm didn't see how the rancher would make that early morning call. And while Longarm had drunk and eaten like a pagan, Spike Drummer's appetite for whiskey and food had put him nearly to shame.

Longarm wasn't quite sure what to do next, but the Shoshone came right back out of Drummer's bedroom and hurried to his side.

"You go to bed with Nita. Have him wake you in morning. Be better for both."

"Look," Longarm said, "I'm damned near engaged to be married."

149

"You hurry to bed with Nita now or he get mad and throw her out. Other men take her then. All take her!"

Longarm understood. Feeling a bit tipsy, he went into the bedroom, stripped down to his underwear and planned on falling asleep beside the Paiute girl.

That wasn't what turned out to happen. Nita was not only awake, but filled with gratitude. She wouldn't stop until she had pulled off Longarm's underwear and then pulled on a few other things too. And before he knew what to do to slow the Paiute girl down, she was on top of him, as wild as a panther.

"I really shouldn't do this. I love Lilly, you see and . . ."

But Nita didn't care anymore about Lilly than the Shoshone woman had. And after a few minutes of her showing her extreme gratitude, Longarm just couldn't restrain himself another minute. His heart was hammering in his chest, his manhood was standing up like a flagpole and, damn his cheatin' hide, he was on that Paiute girl and giving her everything he was worth.

Nita was young, strong and healthy. Longarm wasn't in the habit of making love to Indians, but in the dark and given the desperate circumstances he would be facing with Drummer and his mustangers, he just decided to live for the moment. Actually, it turned out to be a whole lot of moments and every last one of them was fine.

Nita finally let him loose way after midnight, when Longarm was so drained he couldn't offer her another drop of his seed.

She snuggled in close to him, and he put his arm around the young Paiute and kissed her on the lips. "I'm going to do my best to get you out of this fix," he promised. "I'm going to try and set you and the rest of these Indian women free."

Nita said something in her own tongue. Longarm hadn't the faintest idea what it meant but he knew she was still grateful and happy. Even more than that, she had finally been satisfied.

They fell asleep then, and Longarm figured she was probably smiling like he was.

Chapter 18

When Longarm awoke, the sun was already hanging over the rim of the canyon and birds were singing in the pines. Nita was gone, but there was a cup of strong coffee at his bedside. Longarm groaned and sat up, feeling a slight touch of the whiskey damage. He placed his feet on the floor and reached for his coffee. To his surprise and gratification, it was liberally laced with brandy.

"You sleep well?" the Shoshone woman asked, coming into the bedroom with a pot of coffee to refill his cup.

"I expect I'll survive. Where is Nita?"

"Cooking in kitchen. Big smile on face. Says she likes you much better than Jake."

"Glad to hear that," Longarm said, running his fingers through his long hair. "Where is Mr. Drummer?"

"He asleep. Not feel good today." The woman set down her coffeepot and placed both hands on the sides of her head with a low groan.

"I get the picture," Longarm said. "I'm not feeling so hot either and he drank a lot more whiskey than I did last night."

"Men getting ready to ride after mustangs. You go with them?"

"I figure I should," Longarm said, suddenly aware that he was naked. He put his coffee cup down and reached for his underclothes. The Shoshone woman was staring at his manhood, which appeared rather pathetic at this hour of the morning after a hard but enjoyable night's work.

"Excuse me," Longarm said. "But you're staring at it."

"Big."

"Well, uh, it suits me," Longarm said, feeling a bit embarrassed as he hastily drew on his pants. "Listen, I'm coming back and I'll figure a way to get all of you out of this canyon and back to your own people."

Her smile wilted. "They kill you."

"I'm not easy to kill." Longarm finished dressing as he slurped down his second cup of coffee. "I smell bacon or ham frying. I'd better eat before I leave. Got a feeling that eating won't be high on the agenda when we start after mustangs."

" 'Agenda'?"

"You know. It won't be important."

She didn't understand and he didn't have time to explain. Longarm followed the woman into the kitchen, where several Indian women were cooking. When Nita saw him, she smiled almost coyly and made sure that he was seated at the table with a big plate of ham and eggs.

"Much obliged," Longarm told her. Then he winked and added, "You're quite a little woman, Nita."

In reply, she giggled and then reached down to pat his crotch almost lovingly. All the women in the kitchen laughed. Longarm felt his cheeks grow warm. He gulped down his food, after hearing one of the men outside talking loudly on the porch.

"I'd better get going," Longarm told the Indian slave women. "Thanks for breakfast."

To his surprise and dismay, there were at least a dozen men outside, faces that Longarm had not seen before. He picked out Derwin Cooper, who was already on horseback, and went over to the young mustanger. "Who the hell are all these new men?"

"Some of them arrived last night from Elko. The rest just stay here and guard the ranch while we're gone."

"Isn't Mr. Drummer going with us today?"

"No," Derwin said. "He isn't feeling well. Maybe he'll come along later with a few of the others."

Longarm was feeling worse by the minute because, if several of these men had just come from Elko, they'd probably know his true identity. If they did, then he was as good as dead.

"We got Jake's horse saddled for you," Derwin told him. "And that pinto mustang you were riding showed up at the corral."

"He did?"

"Yeah. Mr. Drummer will probably have him shot when he wakes up with his hangover. He's real mean after a night of hard drinking."

"Oh," Longarm said, hoping that Pronto would be wise enough to keep out of the rancher's sight.

"You finally ready to ride?" Derwin asked, not willing to look him in the eye.

Longarm took a deep breath. He might get shot right here and now, but that didn't seem to be their plan, so he said, "I'll be ready just as soon as I get my rifle and ammunition, which I left in the house."

"I don't expect you'll be needing that rifle, mister."

"Derwin, it doesn't matter to me if you think I will need the Winchester or not. I'll be right back."

Derwin shot a look at one of the other men, but said nothing. Longarm marched back into the house, aware that the conversation in the yard had died and that every eye was fixed on his back. He was pretty sure that the men from Elko would have told the others that he was a federal marshal. He was equally sure that he would not be returning to this ranch, because these mustangers would find a way to kill him out in the hills. Someplace where the vultures and coyotes would pick his bones clean.

When he entered the house, Nita was standing in their bedroom, clutching his rifle with both hands so hard that her knuckles were white. She spoke in words he did not understand, but her worry was extreme and very evident.

Then the Shoshone woman hurried in and closed the door behind her so that they were alone for a moment in the bedroom. "You lawman," she whispered. "They *kill* you!"

"I've already figured that out," Longarm said. "I'll be waiting for my chance to kill 'em first."

"Run away fast!"

"I wouldn't get very far," he told the two women. "I'll have to take my chances out there, look for an opening and get the jump on them boys. If there's too many, I'll make a run for it. But I'll be back here somehow or some way. That's a promise I mean to keep as long as I'm breathin'."

The two Indian women hugged him fiercely. Longarm was touched to the heart and he could feel Nita trembling. "I *will* be back," he said again and then he left and marched out to his waiting horse just as confidently as if he were going to church on a bright Sunday morning.

Minutes later, as Longarm was reining after the six mustangers now galloping out of the canyon, he twisted around in his saddle to see Spike Drummer standing naked on his front porch. Off to his right stood Nita and the Shoshone slave. They were all looking at him as if he were already buried.

Longarm turned his back on them and followed the mustangers out of the canyon. He was feeling a mite thick-headed despite the coffee and not all too spry, but he had his Colt, his Winchester rifle and the little hide-out derringer, which was a real corker at close range. Just as importantly, he knew what these men knew . . . that his last hours were to be short, because the odds against him were almost impossibly long.

It wasn't going to be easy, but Longarm had to find a way out of this death trap.

Chapter 19

Most men can feel when they are being constantly watched as if they were prey. Longarm felt that as they rode toward the Ruby Mountains. He tried to stay behind the six mustangers, but they were far better horsemen and somehow managed to keep him in the front of their hunting pack. As the hard-riding hours passed, Longarm could feel tension mounting. He had decided that a man named Tilford was the leader of this bunch, and that he would probably make the first murderous move.

Derwin Cooper was the only one of the six that Longarm thought might have second thoughts about killing him, but Derwin wouldn't dare cross the line and go up against his co-conspirators. Frank, the man that Longarm had kicked in the face and balls, rode with his eyes burning hatred. His face was swollen up so badly that it had distorted his features, and it was mostly purple. Frank would desperately want to kill Longarm slowly.

"Fine day!" Longarm said around noon when they dismounted at a creek to rest their lathered horses. "Hell of a fine day. I'm really looking forward to riding with you gentlemen. Watching how experts catch mustangs. Ought to be real interesting."

"Oh," Tilford said, hobbling his horse and then loosening the cinch, "it will be interesting. Glad you're enjoying the day, mister."

"Custis is my name. Custis Long."

"That a fact?"

"Yes it is. Where you from, Tilford?"

"Here and there. Whichever way the wind blows and the mustangs run, that's where I want to be. And you?"

"West Virginia. Lately, however, I've been visiting down on the Comstock Lode."

"What about Denver, Colorado?" Tilford asked without looking at him. "You ever seen that city?"

Longarm felt sweat trickle down his spine. Everyone in the noon camp had frozen. "As a matter of fact," Longarm replied, "I have been to Denver. It's growing so fast that I hardly recognized the place."

"Yeah, big, big town," Tilford said. "Sure a lot of folks. Too many for me. I like it out here in the open where there's not much sound. Just the wind and the bugs and the birds. Animals killin' or bein' killed. Horses' hooves pounding. A coyote's sorrowful howl. Those are the sounds I most appreciate."

"You're damn near poetic," Longarm said with a smile frozen on his chapped lips.

"Well, as a matter of fact, Custis, I have written a little poetry. And a few eulogies. You know what they are?"

"Sure, words you say when you bury a man. Sometimes they are etched on a fella's gravestone."

"That's right. You see, Custis, I like to read gravestones," Tilford admitted, his eyes taking on a faraway look. "You learn when a man was born and when he died. Some of 'em even say *how* the fella died. It's my observation that most women die of disease, overwork and in childbirth. Men, hell they die of a lot more interesting causes. Gunshots. Stab wounds. Pneumonia. Arrow in the back. Accidents in mines and on horses. Whatever. I find graveyards and headstones real, real interesting."

"I guess they are," Longarm replied, dragging his Winchester from the saddle boot and wondering if they were going to try and kill him right here and now.

Tilford raised his eyebrows in question. "What are you holding that rifle for?"

Longarm smiled as if he were talking to a dear old friend and said, "It's like this, Tilford. Yesterday, Mr. Drummer said that I was to be on a constant lookout for Indians. I told him that I wasn't any good with a rope, and sure wasn't a mustanger so he said my job was to guard the camp. Well, the way I see it, I can't guard you hard-riding boys without being well armed and ready to shoot at the first sign of an Indian, now can I?"

Tilford wasn't pleased. He looked like he'd been sprayed with skunk stink.

"Well, can I now?" Longarm asked a second time.

"I guess not."

If the circumstances had been altogether different, Longarm could have enjoyed himself pulling Tilford's chain. "How long are we staying here in this camp?"

"Maybe an hour. We've got to rest these horses. If we get jumped by Indians or come upon a bunch of mustangs, our mounts have to be fresh and ready to run for all they are worth."

"An hour?" Longarm gazed around as if he did not have a care in the world. He said, "I think I'll go up on that little hill yonder. That would be a good lookout place for me. Don't you agree?"

Tilford said nothing as Longarm detached from the murderous bunch and climbed the rock-strewn hill, where he would be safe for at least the next hour.

The hour passed pleasantly enough. But just as the mustangers started to get off the ground and go to catch the horses, Longarm saw a dust cloud on the horizon. He wondered if it were Indians or mustangs. If it were Indians, maybe it was Chief Niawah's band and they could help him save his hide. But that seemed like too much to hope for.

"Come on down and let's move on!" one of the mustangers shouted.

"I'll be right there." Longarm hesitated, staring hard at the growing cloud of dust.

"Dammit, we're gettin' ready to ride out!" Tilford bellowed. "Quit jackin' around up there!"

Longarm unbuttoned his pants and took a leak. That gave him a minute or two, and by then he could see that the dust cloud was being raised by a small band of mustangs, and that they were probably heading for this very spot to drink.

"Here I come, Tilford," he called down to the impatient bunch. "Sorry to keep you waiting."

Tilford didn't say a word and neither did the other men, until Derwin asked, "Did you see anything up there but birds?"

"I saw a band of wild horses."

"You did!"

"Yep."

"Why the hell didn't you say so?" Tilford asked. "How many?"

"I'd guess there's only about nine or ten."

Tilford swung onto his horse and galloped almost to the top of the hill. He dismounted, keeping himself and his horse just under the skyline. Longarm watched as Tilford removed a pair of binoculars from his saddlebag and studied the approaching mustangs. Satisfied, he put his binoculars away, walked his horse down the hill and said, "Custis is right. It's that same wily band that got away from us last month. Same blue roan stallion leading 'em."

"He's a smart bugger," a mustanger said. "He won't be easy. How we gonna handle this?"

Tilford thought for a long while and then said, "We'll split up and let them come drink this water. We can hide and wait until their bellies are so full they can't run good. Then we bust out and rope them."

"If there's nine or ten and only five of us doin' the ropin', what do we do with the other mustangs?"

"Rope the biggest mares that will bring more at the killers." Tilford glanced at Longarm. "When we jump the band, we'll run 'em by where you're hiding so that you shoot the blue roan. Aim for his shoulder. If you hit and break it, he'll go down quick. If you miss and hit the stud in the belly, he'll still go down kicking even if he manages to run a mile or two before dropping. Understand?"

Longarm wasn't happy. "That's how it's usually done?"

"Look," Tilford explained. "When the stud goes down, his mares will scatter in confusion. They'll smell the blue's blood, hear him thrash and scream. That's when they're easiest to rope, if we all do our job."

Longarm didn't want to gun down the stallion, but he nodded his head as if he were in full agreement. He had the feeling that these men were going to kill him at the first opportunity, but that this band of mustangs had given him a temporary reprieve.

"I'll do it," he said.

"Good. Don't miss."

"Don't worry," Longarm told them mustanger. "I *won't* miss."

"All right, ride your horse up into those rocks, dismount and be ready to plug that blue demon."

Longarm did as he'd been ordered, careful not to expose his back to these men. He could almost feel their excitement, and he supposed it was the same kind of feeling that prospectors experienced when they found a gold nugget or some promising digs. Whatever it was, Longarm was grateful that they had been distracted long enough for him to get up here and think things out while they chased and tried to rope mustangs.

He tried to secure Jake's horse in the rocks, but there wasn't anything solid to tie the big gelding to. Not a bush or pine in sight. Longarm was an improviser, so he tied the reins around a small rock. The rock, of course, wouldn't hold the horse if it chose to break away, but it might fool the animal long enough to keep it hidden.

"Here we go," Longarm said, taking a hiding place and watching as the mustangers disappeared behind cover. He removed his hat and eased his head over the rocks, wanting to get a better view of the "blue demon," as one of the mustangers had dubbed the mustang stallion.

The roan was a fine-looking horse. Maybe a little big-headed and thicker in the neck than most ranch-bred saddle horses. And, as it drew nearer, Longarm could see that it was missing the tip of one ear. No doubt the ear had been bitten off by a rival in a terrible fight for the mares. But despite all that, the stallion possessed a regal bearing, with its thick neck bowed, feet almost dancing on the hard ground and eyes missing nothing that posed a danger.

As the roan drew closer to the creek, it slowed to a walk and dropped its head, weaving it back and forth like a cobra. How fascinating! It was, Longarm realized, looking at the tracks made by him and the mustangers just minutes earlier. The roan stopped and reared up on its back feet. It sounded a warning and the mares stopped cold in their tracks, bunching up in confusion.

Blue Demon, now is when I'm supposed to put a bullet through your shoulder, Longarm thought. *Then I'm supposed to shoot you in the head so that your mares can see you thrashing and dying in agony and become too rattled to run away until the mustangers are on you with their whirling ropes.*

Longarm smiled. The roan stallion was big and well muscled, but scarred badly. *Kinda like I am, aren't you,*

164

Longarm thought. *You don't have just the one mare, either. I expect you like variety. Kinda like I do.*

In that moment, as Longarm watched the wary blue roan stomp and rear and twist its head with rolling eyes, he saw the truth and the connection. *I too can be bitten, cut bloody, scarred and even beaten, but my spirit would never be tamed. Not by any one heart . . . not by any one female.*

"Sorry, Miss Lilly," he said, standing erect so that the mustang stallion could see him clearly. "But it just isn't meant to be. Run, Blue Demon, and take your girls with you!"

"Shoot the sonofabitch!" Tilford screamed across the distance, as he and his men came busting out of the cover. "Shoot him *now!*"

Longarm raised his rifle, aimed and shot Tilford in the chest sending him and his whirling rope somersaulting over the back of his charging horse. The others were running forward toward the band of mustangs with such concentrated intensity that Longarm managed to get off three more clean shots before the last of the men swerved their racing mounts away from his rifle fire and disappeared into the brush. Longarm caught a glimpse of one rider slumped forward in his saddle a moment before the man pitched forward, his horse racing after the others.

The roan stallion was already biting the backsides of his mares and driving them in the opposite direction, toward the tall Ruby Mountains, where the country was so rugged and unmapped that mustangs could hide for years without being caught.

The stud slid to a halt at the top of a barren ridge and looked back across a mile of trees, rocks and brush.

Longarm waved at the animal, his kindred spirit. The scarred and magnificent blue demon reared and bugled a fierce cry of freedom that made Longarm shiver and then grin, despite all the death that he had just dealt.

Chapter 20

When the young mustanger named Derwin Cooper saw Longarm riding up, he made a feeble attempt to unholster his gun and defend himself. But he was badly shot and not much of a killer so Longarm didn't even bother to finish him off.

"Say, Derwin?" Longarm drawled, looking down at the kid from the back of Frank's big mustanging horse.

"Marshal Long, why did you go and shoot me like that?"

Longarm dismounted and stood towering over the kid. "You know why. You were going to kill me."

"I wasn't!" Derwin's face was pale. Longarm could see that he'd lost quite a lot of blood from a rifle bullet to his body.

"You should have sided with me, Derwin. You boys knew that I was a federal marshal when we rode out this morning and you were about to kill me."

"No!"

Longarm drew a cigar from his shirt pocket. He knelt beside the wounded mustanger. "Derwin," he said, "you're probably going to die right here. How old are you?"

"Seventeen. Almost eighteen."

"How'd you fall in with Spike Drummer's murderous bunch of mustangers?"

Derwin swallowed hard. "I . . . I wanted to learn how to catch wild horses."

"So they can be shipped East to the slaughterhouses? Not a very noble thing to do for a living."

The boy shook his head and Longarm brushed a large black ant from the kid's forehead. Derwin wet his lips and said, "Captured mustangs don't always go to the Eastern slaughterhouses. Sometimes, when you catch a really good one, maybe one not too old or set in its wild ways, then you can tame it. Make it into a fine cow pony or good riding horse."

"I'm not too sure of that," Longarm said. "I bought that pinto mustang back in Elko and he bucked me off. Damn near broke me in half."

"You didn't *handle* him right," Derwin said, his eyes filling with tears from the pain he was experiencing. "You need to handle a mustang different than you would a ranch or farm-raised horse. They're scared of men right down in the marrow of their bones. That's why they need lots of extra work and attention. You got to be slower around them. Real, real easy and especially gentle."

Longarm lit his cigar and inhaled deeply. "Is that right?"

"Yes, sir!"

"Well," Longarm said, "I'm not going to go mustanging again. What I want to know right now is who is behind the Elko murders and the railroad robberies."

Derwin's head rolled back and forth in the sand and dirt. "If I tell you, I'm a dead man."

"If you *don't* tell me, I'll leave you here to die anyway. You have only one sensible choice, Derwin. Use your head and tell me everything."

The kid coughed and pleaded for a drink of water from Longarm's canteen. It was given to him and then Longarm unbuttoned Derwin's shirt. A rifle bullet had bored through

168

the mustanger's body, causing a lot of blood loss, but the bullet might not have hit any vital organs. If they'd been in town, even a half decent sawbones could have patched Derwin up and saved his life. But way out here in this rough country . . . well, Longarm gave the kid a fifty-fifty chance at best.

"Derwin, you're leaking," Longarm said matter-of-factly. "Now, tell me who I need to either kill or arrest and don't leave out any names. If you do that, and I believe you, then I'll patch you up and try to get help. Otherwise . . ."

Longarm didn't finish. He didn't need to say another word.

"Marshal, you ought to have it figured out," Derwin gasped. "It's all Mr. Drummer's doin'. He's the one . . . him and Mayor Coleman and Marshal Nestor. And Deputy Coon, along with Tilford and a few of the mustangers."

"Tilford is dead and several of his friends, as well."

"You sure caught us by surprise," the kid said. "And you didn't waste a shot."

"I couldn't afford to," Longarm replied. "I had to whittle down the odds in a hurry."

"You did that all right."

"Derwin, did you ever kill anyone?" Longarm asked, untying his bandana and wondering if he could save the kid.

"No. I'm a terrible shot. I just wanted to find me the perfect wild horse, tame him and ride him all over the country, showin' him off and making myself famous."

Longarm frowned. " 'Famous'? What in the hell are you talking about?"

"I could have ridden a great mustang I'd caught and gentled in Buffalo Bill's Wild West Show. I'd have made a name for myself on that roan stallion we just saw, if he had been younger and not so scarred up. But I was gonna find the *perfect* young mustang stallion, Marshal Long. I was gonna be someone real, real special."

"Maybe," Longarm said, "you should just be yourself and try to stay honest and alive."

"I *am* honest! You gotta believe me." Derwin cried, eyes pleading. "You can't just let me lie here and bleed to death."

"Sure I can . . . but I won't. I'll help you out because I believe what you said about Drummer, the mayor and Elko's marshal. And you might have to testify to their guilt in a court of law."

"I'd do that. What choice do I have?"

"None," Longarm said, looking around and trying to think how he might save this kid.

"Marshal, you have to understand that we can't go back to the ranch. Mr. Drummer will be there and so will the ones that got away just now."

"You'd never survive a trip all the way back to Elko. If we don't go back to that canyon ranch, where else can we go?"

Tears rolled down Derwin's sunken cheeks. "I don't know."

Longarm thought about it for a minute. "We only have one choice and that's to find Chief Niawah's village."

"Holy God, no!" Derwin's eyes were round with fear. "The Paiutes hate us mustangers. They'd torture and scalp us."

"We'll have to take that chance," Longarm decided, ripping his bandana in half. "Now I'm going to plug up these bullet holes with this bandana. Then I'll catch a second horse for you to ride and we'll try to find the Paiutes as fast as possible. Kid, believe me, it's your only hope."

Derwin swallowed hard. "I'm even more scared of the Paiutes than I am of you, Marshal Long. But I suppose that what you're saying makes sense. I got nothing left to lose except my life."

"That's right," Longarm said. "There are times when you just have to go for broke. And that's what we're going to do now."

"Yes, sir," Derwin said, grinding his teeth as Longarm jammed his bandana into the entry and exit wounds.

170

"We're going to make it through this," Longarm promised the kid, with more conviction in his voice than he really felt inside. "So just don't give up, Derwin. Life is short enough as it is without giving up."

"Yes, sir."

Longarm hurried over to his horse. He mounted it and headed off at a trot to find a second mount for Derwin. Maybe the kid would make it, maybe not.

Hell, he thought, *maybe neither of us will see another sunrise.*

Chapter 21

Longarm didn't have to find Chief Niawah because the Paiute chieftain quickly found him. Niawah and a dozen of his warriors had come to fight and kill the mustangers. But when they found out that Longarm had done half their work for them, they were very happy.

"Derwin isn't like the others," Longarm told the chief as they sat beside the creek. "He is a good kid who made some bad mistakes. I want his life to be saved. To prove he is my friend . . . and yours . . . he will help us kill Drummer and his men who are in the canyon's rock house. And he will help us free your women and those of the Shoshone who have been kept by Drummer as slaves."

Niawah said, "Paiute have strong medicine to save your friend."

"Good," Longarm said. "Derwin and I will ride beside you to defeat Spike Drummer and his mustang killers. If any are spared from the fight, I will arrest and take them to the white man's court, where they will be tried for many serious crimes. The ones who hanged your warriors will themselves hang. This is my promise to you, Chief Niawah."

Niawah nodded his head in approval and understanding.

"Listen to me well, lawman. Paiute and Shoshone try many times to go into that place and kill mustangers. Free Indian women. Always many warriors die."

"We'll do things differently this time," Longarm said. "But it will not be easy and some will die."

Niawah thought about this for a long time, then he went to speak to his warriors. Longarm stayed beside Derwin and whispered, "We're still wearing our scalps, aren't we, boy?"

"Yes, sir, but I want to stay with you, Marshal. I won't be sent off to some Indian village. I won't do that!"

Longarm understood Derwin's fear. Alone, it was quite possible that he would be killed by the vengeful Paiutes . . . or at least they would see that he died of his existing bullet wound.

"You must help us attack Drummer and what's left of his riders in the box canyon."

"Do you trust that old chief?"

"I do," Longarm replied. "Niawah is a man of honor. And he believes that I can help him finally put an end to Spike Drummer and his murderous gang."

Derwin swallowed hard. "You just tell me what you want me to do, and if I can, I'll damn sure do it."

"Fair enough," Longarm told the kid.

Niawah returned with another Indian, an older one with streaks of silver in his black hair. Niawah looked at Longarm, then down at the mustanger and grunted, "Strong medicine man."

"Glad to hear it," Longarm said.

The Paiute medicine man was a little scary-looking; his eyes rolled and his hair was matted with pine pitch and stuck out so that he looked as if he were wild and crazy in the head. He wore an Army cavalry shirt, buckskin breeches and a pair of handsome cowboy boots. He also carried six leather pouches and many beads and trinkets made of bones and metal buttons.

Derwin was frightened of the man, but realized that he had no choice but to submit to his ministrations. So the Paiute medicine man prepared a smoky fire and sprinkled it with herbs, then hurried off into the brush and trees to gather fresh ingredients for a healing poultice. It didn't take him long to ready the boiling brew in a blackened bean can.

"What's he doing?" Derwin fretted. "What's he gonna do now?"

"I don't know for sure," Longarm said, "but I think he's going to drop that hot rag on the wound so that it draws out the poison."

"Oh, no!"

"If you cry out in pain," Longarm warned, "these people will think you weak and that the medicine will not help. So, whatever you do, don't scream."

Derwin swallowed hard. "I'm in enough pain already."

"Be brave or you might end up dead," Longarm warned.

As expected, the medicine man dipped a dirty rag into the cauldron and removed the steaming poultice with a pair of sticks. When the poultice was dropped on Derwin's wound, the kid almost screamed, but locked his jaws and managed to keep silent while beads of sweat erupted across his face.

Niawah and the Paiutes were impressed. They didn't say so, but Longarm could see that Derwin had won some respect.

"How soon can this man ride?" Longarm asked, not wanting Spike Drummer to have any more time to prepare his next move than was necessary.

"Ride soon," Niawah said. "Sun go down, we ride to canyon."

"Good," Longarm told the Paiute chief. "And we'll hit them tomorrow morning at dawn."

Niawah nodded in agreement, then he went off and sang what Longarm hoped was not his death song.

• • •

175

In the dark of the night, Longarm and the Paiute warriors used the lariats they had collected from the saddles of the dead mustangers Longarm had shot. There weren't many ropes, but they were just long enough so that Longarm and three of Niawah's best warriors were able to lower themselves down the cliff wall behind the ranch house.

At daybreak, the old Paiute chief and his warriors mounted a fierce frontal attack from the opening of the canyon. Only this time, they stayed just out of rifle range.

"Let's go!" Longarm told the three Indians as they hurried toward the unwatched and unprotected back of the house.

Longarm and the Paiutes entered the rock house through an open window, hearing Drummer shouting orders and his men firing their weapons. Suddenly, Drummer's Shoshone slave woman appeared. When she saw Longarm and the Paiutes with guns ready, she led them out of the room and down the hallway.

Nita appeared with a pair of pistols. Before Longarm could say a word, several more Indian slaves appeared from the kitchen with boning knives clenched in their fists.

Longarm knew that knives were useless against guns. Still, in an all-out attack across the front room, there would be more than enough Indians to overcome Drummer and his men.

"Freeze!" Longarm called as he jumped into the big room. "You're all under arrest!"

Drummer whirled, his face reflecting shock and amazement. He held a rifle and when he raised the weapon, Longarm shot him in the head. There were six or seven other men with rifles, and they made the mistake of putting up a fight.

The Indian slaves attacked with a fury that was damn near unbelievable. Nita was shot and killed and the Shoshone woman went down with a bullet in her arm. But by then the mustangers were buried by furious kitchen slaves and Paiute warriors. The light was dim, the early morning air chill, but Longarm would never forget the terrible slaughter. He could do nothing but watch, because any bullets he unleashed might hit the incensed Indians.

The fight wasn't really a fight at all. It was a bloodbath that made Longarm turn away and leave the house seeking fresh, cold air.

Chief Niawah took the young Paiute woman away to his people for burial. His medicine man was successfully treating Spike Drummer's Shoshone woman and several other Indians who had been wounded in the savage assault.

Longarm didn't object when the Indians sacked and burned everything inside the rock house. They also torched the bunkhouse and even the corrals where Longarm found Pronto penned with other horses. The Paiutes were filled with such deep hatred for Drummer that they dragged his corpse out into the yard and hanged it from a pine bough.

The Indians who had been household slaves bathed in the creek that gurgled from the base of the back canyon wall. They burned their household clothing, preferring to wear saddle blankets and skins. Everyone feasted for two days on the food from Drummer's pantry. Then they prepared to leave for the Rubys.

"White men will come now and kill us," Niawah said, sadness in his voice.

"No," Longarm told the old chief. "I will say that I did this thing alone."

Niawah's face reflected doubt. "Alone?"

"With Derwin. I am a United States marshal and these men were hated by the townspeople of Elko. My story will not be questioned, and the people will be glad that this is finished."

Niawah thought about this for several minutes. Then he said, "Come with us, tall lawman. Come live with our people and be free."

"I can't," Longarm told the chief. "I still have a job to do. My work is not done."

"There are others?"

"Three more," Longarm replied. "Elko's mayor, marshal and deputy."

Niawah looked relieved. "Then we come and help you!"

"No," Longarm said. "That would only do harm to your people. I will do this business by myself."

The chief looked over at Derwin. "That boy help you?"

"Maybe."

"You great warrior. You will kill them *all.*"

"I will if they resist being arrested."

"Marshal Long?"

He turned to see Derwin standing beside the corral. "I want to ride your pinto mustang into Elko."

"Why?"

"Because he is a mustang and a pretty damn good-looking horse."

"But he won't make you famous," Longarm said. "He's not the flashy stallion you were going to tame and ride in a Wild West show."

"No, he isn't" Derwin admitted. "But I heard what you told the chief; that I helped you kill Drummer and all his men. *That* will make me famous. Almost as famous as yourself."

Longarm started to tell the kid that that kind of fame wasn't the kind he needed, but decided to do it later.

"You're in no shape to get bucked off by Pronto."

"He won't buck me off," Derwin vowed. "I'll explain things to him. Tell him how it will be from now on, if you let me buy him from you."

"Help me out in Elko by testifying against the guilty officials, and he's my gift to you," Longarm said.

Derwin nodded in agreement and said, "I guess since you almost shot me dead yesterday that is the very least you should do."

Longarm laughed.

Chapter 22

The circuit judge glared down at former mayor John Coleman, former town marshal Orvis Nestor and former deputy Don Coon. "The people of Nevada have spoken. You are all three judged guilty of extortion, accessory to murder and the theft of government bonds. Therefore, I sentence you to hang by the necks until dead."

The former mayor collapsed, sobbing, on his knees. The former town marshal screamed a curse at the judge, the jury and especially at Longarm. Don Coon, the deputy, just buried his homely face in his hands and wept like a baby.

The crowd that filled the little courtroom was silent, their expressions pitiless and hard.

Longarm's work in Elko was finished. He hurried outside with Derwin on his heels, just wanting to go someplace, anyplace.

"Marshal Long?"

He turned to see Ervin Duncan, better known in this town as E. P. or "Excellent Person."

"Yeah?"

"I didn't want to disturb you during the sentencing today, but you have an important telegram from Denver."

Longarm stuck out his hand. Since he had been forced

to remain in Elko for nearly a month because of the highly publicized trial, he expected this to be additional funds from his boss, Billy Vail.

Instead, the telegram was from Miss Lilly. "Excuse me," Longarm said, turning to walk away so that he could read the message in private.

"My condolences, Marshal Long," E. P. called out. "I'm *really* sorry."

Longarm tore open the telegram and read:

Dear Custis,

> *You have been gone two months and haven't even written me even a line. I have decided not to marry you. I have found another, better man which makes both me and my parents extremely happy.*

Lilly

"Marshal Long?"

It was Derwin, hat in hand. "Is it real bad news, sir?"

Longarm gave it only a moment's thought and then he replied, "No, it's . . . it's all right."

"Are you sure?"

"Uh-huh."

"Are you heading back to Denver on the first train?"

Longarm shook his head. "I think I'll go find some tall green mountains and fish for a month. Do you like to fish, Derwin?"

"Yes, sir! But I'm not very good at it."

"Then I'll teach you how to be good at it," Longarm said. "And you can teach me how to win the heart of that pinto mustang."

"Wherever we go, people will know we're famous."

Longarm almost chuckled. "No they won't, kid. Where we're going to fish, nobody will know us at all."

Derwin's smile faded. "Are you sure?"

"I'm sure," Longarm said. "And I'm glad of it. So, if you're still looking for fame, you'd better get on Pronto and go down your own path."

Derwin's brow furrowed. "Think I'd rather have you teach me how to fish real good, Marshal Long."

"Then, Derwin, you're a hell of a lot smarter than I'd thought," Longarm told the kid as he headed down the street toward Miss Bonnie Bucker's saloon.

Watch for

LONGARM AND THE LUNATIC

318th novel in the exciting LONGARM series
from Jove

Coming in May!

**Explore the exciting Old West with one
of the men who made it wild!**

GIANT-SIZED ADVENTURE FROM AVENGING ANGEL LONGARM.

LONGARM AND THE DEADLY DEAD MAN
0-515-13547-X

LONGARM AND THE BARTERED BRIDES
0-515-13834-7

J. R. ROBERTS

THE GUNSMITH